THE RETURN OF MR. BUDD

Near Avernley in Berkshire, Superintendent Budd of Scotland Yard is relaxing on holiday at the cottage of his friend, Jacob Mutch. However, Mr. Budd becomes involved in an investigation. He learns from Jacob's neighbour that his cottage has been burgled — twice. Yet nothing was taken. Then the man is found in his cottage brutally murdered. And the following day, the body of a known criminal is found dead nearby, shot through the head!

Books by Gerald Verner
in the Linford Mystery Library:

THE LAST WARNING
DENE OF THE SECRET SERVICE
THE NURSERY RHYME MURDERS
TERROR TOWER
THE CLEVERNESS OF MR. BUDD
THE SEVEN LAMPS
THEY WALK IN DARKNESS
THE HEEL OF ACHILLES
DEAD SECRET
MR. BUDD STEPS IN

GERALD VERNER

THE RETURN OF MR. BUDD

Complete and Unabridged

LINFORD
Leicester

First published in Great Britain

First Linford Edition
published 2012

British Library CIP Data

Verner, Gerald.
   The return of Mr. Budd. - -
(Linford mystery library)
1. Budd, Robert (Fictitious character)- -
Fiction. 2. Detective and mystery stories.
3. Large type books.
I. Title II. Series
823.9′12–dc23

ISBN 978–1–4448–0971–8

Published by
F. A. Thorpe (Publishing)
Anstey, Leicestershire

Set by Words & Graphics Ltd.
Anstey, Leicestershire
Printed and bound in Great Britain by
T. J. International Ltd., Padstow, Cornwall

This book is printed on acid-free paper

To
Leonard R. Gribble
'The best of good fellows'

THE CLUE
OF THE
WHISPERING PINES

1

Mr. Budd takes a holiday

Joe Rennett was an artist. Even Scotland Yard agreed on this, albeit reluctantly, for during six weary and harassed years, worried officials had watched his activities with increasing despair.

His coups were well thought out and spectacular, and organised to the smallest detail.

During the period he was operating he got away with thousands of pounds in paper money and never once was he caught. When the Wandsworth branch of the British Trust Bank was broken into and the entire contents of the strongroom cleared, it was as obviously Rennett's work as if he had scrawled his signature across the shattered door of the open vault. But when they went to pull him in he only smiled and produced an unshakable alibi. He had spent the night at

3

Barnes, sitting up with a sick friend, and brought forward four witnesses, including a doctor and a nurse, to prove it.

'You can't be clever all the time, Rennett,' growled the disgruntled Inspector who had come to take him. 'One of these fine days we'll get you.'

Joe grinned — he was proud of his teeth, which were all his own in spite of his fifty-seven years.

'You'll never get me!' he declared, boastingly. 'Neither on a fine day nor a wet day. You've been trying for five years and you'll never do it.'

And he was right, for they never did.

When the Inspector reported his failure to Mr. Budd, that large and somnolent man shook his head wearily.

'He's got an army of people workin' with him,' he remarked, 'and he can afford to pay 'em well. The only hope we've got is to catch him out on one of his alibis or else get him red-handed, and I think he's too clever for either.'

It was exactly a year later when Mr. Rennett threw his last and most spectacular coup.

Between five o'clock on a Saturday afternoon and three o'clock on a Sunday morning the American Exchange Bank of New York's London office was robbed of five hundred thousand dollars. The robbery was discovered by a patrolling policeman who failed to get an answer to the usual signal arranged with the officials of the bank. He notified his station and when the detectives arrived they found the night watchman securely tied up in the manager's office, the lock of the strongroom burnt out, and the cases that contained the bills gone.

An examination of the watchman proved of little help. The man had seen nothing of the robbers. He had been making his rounds late on the Saturday night when somebody had sprung on him as he was walking through a passage. A cloth had been thrown over his head and that was all he knew.

The cloth was found lying on the floor in the room where he had been made prisoner and it still reeked of the drug that had been used.

The whole thing had obviously been

5

planned very carefully, since the constable who had made the discovery had had no suspicion until he failed to get the usual reply to his signal just after three o'clock. This consisted of two short burrs on a buzzer situated behind a grille at the side of the main door, and was supposed to be given every hour in reply to the constable pressing a small bell-push which operated a similar buzzer in the watchman's room.

The inference was evident. The thieves must have been aware of the arrangement and put one of their number on to deal with it while the rest were cutting out the lock of the strongroom door.

Mr. Budd, when he arrived, looked at the scene of the robbery sleepily and uttered one word — 'Rennett!' Detectives were sent out to find the smiling Joe and pull him in. The stout Superintendent went back to the Yard to await their return, speculating on what form Mr. Rennett's alibi would take this time.

But Joe Rennett could not be found. He was not at any of his usual haunts, neither had anything been seen of him at the sedate flat which he rented in Maida

Vale. He had left on the Saturday morning saying that he was spending the weekend in the country, and since then his old and decrepit servant had heard nothing from him.

A policeman was left in charge of the premises and to keep an eye on the tearful old woman who had supplied this information, and the search for the missing Mr. Rennett continued.

He was found at two o'clock on the Monday afternoon in the mortuary at Catering, a small village on the Staines Road, and his injuries were so severe that identification was rendered difficult. His body had been discovered by a labourer on his way to work, lying near a twisted and mangled motorcycle. An inspection of the scene of the accident, which was a lane connecting the main road with a secondary thoroughfare, suggested that Rennett had met his death by a violent collision with another motor vehicle. There were marks of tyres on the muddy surface and a patch of black oil showing that a car had stopped.

When the matter was reported to Mr.

Budd he frowned thoughtfully through the smoke of the cigar that was clamped between his teeth.

'He said he'd never be caught,' he murmured, 'and he never will be. I wonder who ran him down and what happened to the money?'

Every effort was made to find an answer to both these questions, but none was forthcoming. The driver of the car that had jerked Joe Rennett into eternity was never found and the five hundred thousand dollars had disappeared as completely as if they had never existed.

During the months that followed, Joe Rennett's last exploit grew dimmer and dimmer in Mr. Budd's mind, though occasionally he would draw forth the dossier containing a list of that enterprising man's activities and glower at it. But the line of red ink stating curtly, 'This man died as the result of a motor accident, September 10th, 1935', in his own big handwriting supplied an effectual finish to the matter.

When, in the late summer of the following year, he started on the last week of a protracted holiday, Joe Rennett and the proceeds of his last robbery had faded almost completely from his mind.

Mr. Budd was in the habit of forming all kinds of queer friendships and one of the queerest was that which he had struck up with old Jacob Mutch. Mr. Mutch was a jobbing gardener when he was anything, which was not often, for he preferred to talk over a pipe and a pint of beer than suffer the indignities of manual labour, and their acquaintanceship had been the outcome of the stout Superintendent's passion for roses.

Mr. Mutch lived in a cottage on the outskirts of the village of Avernley, which sprawls picturesquely on the borders of Berkshire, and from June to late October his garden was ablaze with the flowers Mr. Budd loved. Passing the cottage on his return from an interview with the local Inspector concerning a much-wanted ladder-larcenist who had been operating in the district, the big man stopped to admire, and seeing Mr. Mutch engaged in his usual occupation of drinking beer and smoking in the porch had got into conversation.

He soon discovered that so far as roses were concerned he had found a kindred spirit.

His holiday that year was spent as a paying guest under the hospitable roof of Mr. Mutch and his elderly but still buxom wife. When he reluctantly returned to the Yard, after a hectic fortnight of greenfly and fertilisers, Mr. Mutch had extended a hearty invitation to come again.

The August sun was sending long shadows across the countryside, when the stout Superintendent brought his dingy and noisy little car to a stop at the white gate of the cottage and squeezed himself laboriously from behind the wheel. Mr. Mutch was sitting in his small porch and might, from his appearance, never have moved since Mr. Budd had last seen him. Knowing his habits the stout detective thought it quite probable that he hadn't. A mug of beer was gripped in the gnarled fingers of his right hand, and his short, black, clay pipe was stuck between his few remaining teeth.

He was talking to a tall, thin, elderly man with a hatchet face and a stooping back.

10

'Glad to see 'e, Mr. B,' he greeted, which was his invariable method of addressing the big man. ''Ow are them roses of yours?'

'They might be better an' they might be worse, Jacob,' said Mr. Budd, sniffing appreciatively the perfume from Mr. Mutch's blooms which drenched the evening air. 'You can't grow flowers in a London suburb like you can in the country.'

'No, that's right,' agreed the tall, thin man. 'I lived in Lunnon for a good many years before I came down here an' I could never get nothin' to grow real 'ealthy.'

Mr. Mutch waved the clay pipe that he had taken from between his lips towards the speaker.

'This is Bob Smillit,' he said. ''E's taken that there empty cottage in Thorn Lane which I showed you the last time you was 'ere. Meet Sup'intendent Budd, of Scotland Yard, Bob. I 'spect you'll see a good bit of 'im, 'e's stayin' for a week with me and the Missus.'

'Glad to meet you, sir.' Mr. Smillit held out a horny hand. 'P'raps as you're a detective you'll be able to catch the burglars wots been breakin' into my cottage.'

'Now you don't want to go troublin' Mr. B with that!' broke in old Jacob. ''E's down 'ere on a 'oliday, an' besides, it's Sergeant Buckles' job.'

'Had a burglary, Mr. Smillit?' inquired Mr. Budd.

'Two!' replied Mr. Smillit. 'Two durin' the last six weeks, if you can call 'em burglaries. Nothin' was took.'

'It's some of the village lads 'avin' a game with you,' growled Mr. Mutch. 'Real burglars don't break into a place an' take nothin'.'

'Well, they made enough mess, anyway,' grunted his friend, 'even if they didn't take nothin'. You never seen such a muddle as the place was in.'

Mrs. Mutch appeared from the inside of the cottage at that moment to greet Mr. Budd and announce that supper was ready, and the thin Bob Smillit took his leave.

In the interest of discussing a reliable means for combating mould upon climbers, which filled the time between the end of the meal and bed, the fat man forgot all about Mr. Smillit and his two burglaries.

He was specifically reminded of it on the following morning, however, when Mrs. Mutch woke him up from a dreamless sleep with an early cup of tea. Her face was flushed to an even ruddier hue with excitement and she was so full of her news that she failed to respond to his husky 'Good morning.'

'Oh, Mr. Budd,' she said breathlessly, 'such a dreadful thing has 'appened durin' the night.'

'Eh, what's that?' asked the fat man, blinking at her sleepily.

'You remember Bob Smillit?' she said rapidly. ''Im wot was talkin' to Jacob when you got here last evenin'?'

Mr. Budd hoisted himself on to one elbow and grasped the cup of tea which looked in imminent danger of being upset.

'What about him?' he grunted.

''E's been murdered in his cottage!' said the woman. 'His 'ead bashed in and the place turned upside down!'

Mr. Budd, suddenly very wide awake, stared at her, and then he sighed.

'Don't seem to be able to get away from murders and violence,' he murmured sadly. 'All right, Mrs. Mutch, I think I'll get up.'

2

The footprint in the garden

At first glance Thorn Lane has no visible excuse for existence. Beginning boldly and with some pretentiousness, it straggles indeterminately through a small pine wood and ends abruptly amid a tangle of bushes and apparently leads nowhere. There was a time, however, in the early history of Avernly when it could claim some degree of importance for in those days it was used by the workmen who laboured in the big gravel pits long since disused. The pits themselves are still there but the deposits of gravel have petered out. The workings are given over to weeds and stunted bushes that grow in profusion over the floor and walls of the pits, and so effectively conceal their presence that Thorne Lane is a danger to the unwary and to strangers.

The board that rose from among the bushes with its message of warning of the precipice beyond was practically useless, since long exposure to sun and rain had almost completely obliterated its words. Some attempt had been made to guard the lip of the quarry with a wire fence, but this was broken, and offered little in the way of protection. Not that many people ventured beyond the confines of the little pine wood, for the place had a bad reputation among the villagers, and few strangers were sufficiently impressed to explore.

Pine Cottage was sited about halfway down the lane itself and within a few yards of the beginning of the wood. It stood back in a little rectangle of garden, its white gate dividing the thick, blackthorn hedge which surrounded it. It was a pretty old place, rather dilapidated but still habitable, built of whitewashed brick with a red-tiled roof on which patches of moss stood out greenly.

When Mr. Budd made his way ponderously towards the gate he saw a knot of people collected in the lane whispering excitedly, and by the tiny porch the blue-clad figure of a red-faced policeman.

At the big man's approach the chattering tongues of the sightseers were hushed and a whisper ran from lip to lip. Mr. Mutch was proud of his acquaintanceship with an official of Scotland Yard and the majority of the villagers were aware of Mr. Budd's appearance and rank. As he reached the white gate and laid his hand on the latch a thin man in the uniform of a sergeant of police came out of the open front door behind the constable. The worried frown that darkened his wooden features lifted as he saw Mr. Budd and he hurried quickly down the uneven stone path.

'Good morning, sir,' he said, touching his hat. 'So you've heard about this business, eh?'

Mr. Budd nodded.

'Yes,' he answered in his slow, drawling way. 'Hope I'm not intrudin', Buckle, but I thought I'd come round and have a look.'

'I shall be only too glad of your help, sir,' said Sergeant Buckle fervently. 'I'm not used to this sort of thing and I'm more or less in charge until the Superintendent gets here from Reading.'

Mr. Budd nodded again, his sleepy eyes moving from side to side.

'If I can help you at all I'll be only too pleased,' he murmured. 'Unofficially, of course. I don't want to do anythin' that'll upset the dignity of the County Police.'

Sergeant Buckle removed his hat and with a large handkerchief wiped his perspiring forehead.

'I expect the Chief Constable'll be only too glad of your assistance, sir,' he said. 'Perhaps you'd care to come inside.'

For answer the stout Superintendent opened the gate and together they made their way up the short path. The constable stood aside as they reached the porch, and Buckle led the way into the dark little hall. It was more of a passage than anything else. Facing them a narrow staircase led upwards and on either side was a door, which opened into the two ground floor rooms of the cottage. By the side of the staircase the passage narrowed, evidently leading to the kitchen at the back. The meagre amount of furniture, consisting of an old chest and a hat rack, had been shifted to one side, as had the threadbare rug, which had evidently originally covered the ancient flooring.

Mr. Budd commented on this, and Sergeant Buckle pursed his lips.

'Nothing to what the rest of the rooms are like, sir,' he remarked. 'You'd think there'd been a blinkin' earthquake!'

The big man rubbed his chin gently.

'How was the discovery made?' he asked.

'By the woman what comes in to clean,' answered the sergeant. 'Smillit looked after himself most of the time, but three days a week Mrs. Gimble used to come in for a couple of hours in the mornin' and give a general tidy up. It was 'er what found 'im. It's queer because this ain't the first time there's been trouble at this place. Poor Smillit 'ad burglars twice — '

'And nothin' was taken,' murmured Mr. Budd interrupting the sergeant to the latter's surprise. 'Yes, he was tellin' me that last night. He was talkin' to old Jacob Mutch when I arrived. Where was he found?'

'In here.' Sergeant Buckle pushed open

the door on the right and squeezed himself up against the jamb to make room for the Superintendent's bulky figure.

Mr. Budd crossed the threshold and his face hardened slightly as his eyes took in the scene beyond.

The room was not large and there was not a great deal of furniture. What there was had been dragged into the centre of the floor and left anyhow so that the place presented more the appearance of a salesroom than anything else. Near the fireplace sprawled the thin figure of the man whom Jacob Mutch had introduced him to the previous evening.

He was dressed in an old pair of flannel pyjamas, rather on the small side, so that his bony ankles and wrists protruded grotesquely. He lay face downwards and the back of his head was such an unpleasant sight that even Mr. Budd, who was used to such things, experienced a momentary qualm in the pit of his stomach.

'A nasty murder,' he grunted. 'A nasty, untidy murder. What did they hit him with?'

'I don't know,' said Buckle. 'We can't find any trace of the weapon.'

Mr. Budd pinched the loose flesh of his chin between a fat thumb and finger.

'Queer business, as you say,' he remarked. 'Has the doctor seen him yet?'

The sergeant shook his head.

'No, I'm waiting for 'im now,' he answered. 'He was out on a case when we got through to his place, but they're sendin' 'im up directly he gets back.'

The big man took a step farther into the room.

'You say the rest of the place is like this?' he enquired, and again Buckle nodded.

'In a worse mess,' he said. 'The bedroom 'as been properly pulled to pieces, so has the other room across the passage.'

The Superintendent frowned. Here was obviously no ordinary murder and robbery. To start with, professional burglars would have passed by the unpretentious looking Pine Cottage without a second glance, and this was not the first time it had been broken into. This was the last of three! Smillit had been killed because he had interrupted the marauders at their work, but what was their work? What had attracted them to this tiny house so obviously the habitation of a poor man?

He put a question to the sergeant and Buckle smiled.

'No, sir, Bob Smillit had no money,' he said. 'Only a small pension from the Waterworks. There was nothin' of Smillit's that 'ud pay for their trouble.'

'Then what were they lookin' for?' grunted Mr. Budd. 'They was lookin' for somethin', that's evident, and they've been lookin' for it for a mighty long time. This is the third effort. Let's see the rest of the place.'

Sergeant Buckle conducted him over the small house, and everywhere there was evidence of the intruders' presence. The room opposite the one in which the dead man lay had suffered in the same way. From the appearance of the furniture it had obviously been a sort of 'best parlour', but now it looked like a junk shop. A small, old-fashioned book-case had been denuded of its ancient volumes and a tiny bureau broken open and the contents scattered. The bedroom had been subjected to the same rigorous search, and even the kitchen and the cellar had not been passed over.

The means by which the burglars had effected an entrance interested the big man. A window in the little wash-house-scullery had had one of its panes of glass neatly cut out near the catch and the small circle lay on the ground beneath, a lump of putty still adhering to the centre.

'Nothing amateur about the people who did this,' commented Mr. Budd.

He opened the back door went out and inspected the putty and the ground in the vicinity of the damaged window. The soft earth had been carefully raked over and the indentations on the putty showed that the man who had handled it had been wearing gloves.

'A professional job,' he concluded, with pursed lips, 'and professionals don't waste their time on places like this. How long has Smillit been livin' here?'

'Matter of nine months,' answered Buckle. ''E used to live on the other side of the village in a little row of 'ouses what's been condemned by the Council. When they told 'im he had to get out 'e took this place and sold 'is furniture, what little 'e 'ad.'

'Sold his furniture, eh?' said Mr. Budd. 'Meanin', I suppose, he took this place furnished?'

'That's right,' said the sergeant.

'Who owns it?' asked the Superintendent, and Buckle looked nonplussed.

'Well, I don't rightly know,' he answered. 'It used to belong to a feller what only spent part of his time 'ere, weekends in the Summer. Then 'e didn't come no more, and after a time the estate people shoved up a board 'To Let, Furnished', and that's all I really knows about it.'

Mr. Budd rubbed the side of his nose.

'I think it would be worth while your finding out a bit more,' he said. 'Since, from what you say, these people can't have been after anything belonging to Smillit, it's more than likely they were after somethin' belongin' to the previous tenant. I think it would be worth while your findin' out who this feller was who used to come down for weekends in the Summer and suddenly didn't come any more.'

He was interrupted by the appearance of the constable.

'Doctor Carr's just arrived, sir,' said the man.

'All right, Whittle, I'll come along,' said the sergeant. 'You comin', sir?'

Mr. Budd shook his head.

'No,' he answered. 'I've got nothin' to do with this, Buckle, this is your job. I'm only just nosin' round. I'll have a look at the garden.'

The sergeant retreated into the house with the constable, and the big man stood for a second or two breathing in the soft, sweet smelling air laden with the scent of the nearby pines. It was, as he had said, nothing to do with him. He was on holiday. But at the same time his curiosity had been aroused. It was this that had prompted him to come along and see for himself what had happened after Mrs. Mutch imparted the news.

Pine Cottage was a pleasant spot, he thought; quite a nice little property, with the pine wood to give it a picturesque setting. He ambled slowly down the cinder path beside a mixed border, stopping to sniff the scent from a standard rose tree, and then he saw, in the soft mould of the bed in which it grew, the imprint of a shoe. It was a small print. A tiny sole, with the deeper impression of a horseshoe shaped heel — the print of a woman's high heeled shoe.

He stooped with difficulty. It was not the type of print Mrs. Gimble would leave. The shoe had been worn by a dainty foot. He straightened, his face a little redder. Perhaps it had nothing to do with the crime that had been committed during the night, but it was worth drawing Buckle's attention to all the same. There was only one print. The person who had made it had evidently stepped off the cinder path, perhaps accidentally in the dark.

Mr. Budd retraced his steps and near the house he made his second discovery. A little patch of white attracted his attention, lying near the leafy foliage of a clump of phlox. He hadn't seen it before because on the downward journey the leaves concealed it. He picked it up, a sodden ball of cambric and lace. A woman's handkerchief. He searched the corners for initials, but there were none.

Entering the cottage by the back door he made his way to the room where, from the sound of voices, he guessed he would find Buckle. The sergeant was talking to a young, fair-haired man whom he introduced as Doctor Carr.

'The doctor says, as near as he can tell,' went on the sergeant, 'poor Smillit died between two and three.'

'I can't be certain,' said the fair-haired man pleasantly. 'But that's round about the time.'

'What time did it rain last night?' asked Mr. Budd.

'Rain, sir?' Buckle looked bewildered. 'Did it rain?'

'It did,' said the doctor, 'and I can tell you what time because I was out in it ushering the son and heir of Mrs. Bellows into the world. It started to rain at two o'clock and it left off at twenty past.'

'Thank you,' murmured Mr. Budd. He

held out his big hand. 'I found this near the house in a flower bed,' he said, 'and there's the imprint of a woman's shoe on the edge of another flower bed halfway down the path. Perhaps you could discover who it belongs to?'

'A woman?' exclaimed the surprised Buckle, and Mr. Budd nodded.

His sleepy eyes were watching the doctor whose face, at sight of the handkerchief, had gone suddenly pale.

3

The man with the beard

Superintendent McNeill, a big, raw-boned Scotchman, arrived from Reading just as Mr. Budd was on the point of taking his departure. He was accompanied by an army of satellites, among whom were a fingerprint expert and a police photographer. Sergeant Buckle introduced him to the big man, and McNeill was polite but obviously unimpressed.

'I don't think this is a matter for the Yard, Superintendent Budd — ' he began pompously.

'Neither do I,' broke in Mr. Budd with a yawn, 'and if it was I shouldn't be handlin' it. I'm on a holiday.'

He said goodbye to Buckle and moved ponderously down the little path to the cottage gate. As he emerged into the lane he saw a plump, pleasant-faced little man just getting out of a small two-seater car.

Mr. Thrussel, the manager of the Avernly Branch of the Southern Counties Bank, came towards him. They had met on Mr. Budd's previous visit to the village for Mr. Mutch occasionally did odd jobs in Mr. Thrussel's garden.

'This is a terrible business, a dreadful business!' said the bank manager in his throaty, slightly pontifical manner. 'Avernly has never had such a sensation.'

'No, I don't suppose it has,' agreed Mr. Budd, searching in his pocket for one of his inevitable black cigars. 'I don't suppose it has, Mr. Thrussel.'

'Have the police discovered anything?' went on the fat little man. 'Is there any clue to the person responsible for this atrocious crime?'

'The investigations have only just properly begun,' answered the Superintendent evasively. 'They've been waitin' for the arrival of the officer from Readin'. Now he's taken charge of the proceedin's I expect we shall see things move pretty quick.'

'You mean McNeill?' said the bank manager, and answered his own question by nodding quickly. 'Yes, a very capable man, I believe, I met him once in connection with some slight trouble at the bank, a question of a forged cheque. He struck me then as being a very smart officer.'

'He's so smart,' murmured Mr. Budd without enthusiasm, 'that I shouldn't be surprised if half the village wasn't under arrest by this afternoon.'

Mr. Thrussel looked startled.

'Good gracious!' he exclaimed. 'You're not serious? You don't imagine that — that a local person is responsible for this outrage surely?'

'I don't imagine nothin'!' said the big man, carefully lighting his cigar. 'I'm not in this business at all, except as a looker-on. I'm just spendin' a pleasant holiday. But what McNeill 'ull start imaginin' is quite another matter.'

The bank manager was obviously surprised.

'I should have thought,' he said, coughing slightly as some of the acrid fumes from Mr. Budd's atrocious cigar got into his throat, 'that as you were on the spot you would have taken charge.'

'It doesn't work like that,' explained the Superintendent, shaking his head. 'Scotland Yard can't interfere outside the Metropolitan radius unless it's asked, and I should think that nothin's less likely than that McNeill would want any interference.'

Mr. Thrussel moved out of the range of the rank smoke into more breathable air.

'It's almost impossible to realize that such a dreadful thing as murder could have taken place in such pleasant surroundings,' he declared in a hushed voice, looking towards the sun-lit cottage. 'A beautiful spot, Mr. — er — Superintendent, on a Summer's day, with the breeze whispering through the pines.'

The lids of Mr. Budd's eyes, which had drooped, suddenly shot upwards.

'With the breeze whisperin' through the pines,' he repeated softly and removing his cigar, gently scratched the corner of his mouth with his middle finger. 'Yes, you're right, Mr. Thrussel. It's a pretty place. A very pretty place.'

His eyes had assumed their habitual

sleepy expression.

'Poor Smillit was always saying — Good morning, Miss Brade!' The bank manager broke off in the middle of his sentence to raise his hat politely. Following the direction of his glance Mr. Budd saw a girl standing alone near the beginning of the lane.

She was slight and fair and might have been lovely if it had not been for the unnatural pallor of her face. She acknowledged Mr. Thrussel's greeting with a faint smile, and then looked quickly away.

'Extraordinary how the most unlikely people will flock to anything sensational,' said the bank manager. 'I should never have thought this sort of thing would have held any attraction for Olivia Brade.'

'Who is she?' asked Mr. Budd concealing a yawn.

'She — well, she's — ' Mr. Thrussel appeared to find some difficulty in answering the question. 'I don't know how I can describe her except that she's a resident of Avernly.'

The big man seemed to have lost interest, for he made no attempt to

33

continue the subject. His large face assumed a bored expression and after a moment or two, with a murmured apology, Mr. Thrussel left him and went over to speak to the girl.

Mr. Budd ambled slowly away, a picture of sleepy contentment, but behind that lazy, rather bovine exterior, was a brain that was working rapidly. What elusive memory had those innocuous words of Mr. Thrussel's stirred to semi-consciousness? 'With the breeze whispering through the pines'. Where had he heard that phrase before?

He moved slowly and ponderously along the road towards Mr. Mutch's cottage trying vainly to recollect the circumstances. It was a hackneyed phrase enough, the sort of phrase that a man like Thrussel would use almost subconsciously. And yet it touched a cell in Mr. Budd's brain and set free a recollection that was far removed from Avernly.

He battled with it unsuccessfully. It was like a name that hovered on the tip of his tongue and yet defied utterance. Some time, at some period, he had heard those words before, perhaps not exactly in the order in which the bank manager had said them, and they were connected with a very important incident, an incident which he would have given a great deal to have remembered.

He was still trying to force his mental record to divulge its secret when he reached the cottage. Mr. Mutch was sitting in his favourite seat in the porch and although he was minus his usual mug of beer the clay pipe was well in evidence. He removed it from his lips as Mr. Budd came up the path.

'Your breakfast's been ready for the past hour, Mr. B,' he greeted. 'I've 'ad mine and the Missus is keepin' yours 'ot.'

'Sorry, Jacob,' said the Superintendent. 'I've just been having a look round Smillit's place.'

Mr. Mutch launched into a flood of questions. He was as interested as anybody in the village concerning the murder, but his rooted objection to unnecessary movement of any kind had prevented him from making one of the sightseers that congregated outside

35

the scene of the crime.

Mr. Budd was doing his best to satisfy the old man's curiosity when Mrs. Mutch interrupted him by calling for him to 'come and eat his breakfast at once unless he wanted it burnt to a cinder.'

The big man retired to the cool interior of the cottage and ate his meal, to the accompaniment of a running fire of further questions from the lady of the house.

When he had finished his breakfast he made an excuse and went upstairs to his room, for although he had reiterated that the affair was nothing to do with him, and that he had no wish to spoil his holiday by becoming involved in it, he was intensely interested.

What lay behind this killing of an unpretentious man like Bob Smillit? A harmless, elderly workman living on a pension drawn from the Waterboard. What was the reason for there having been three separate attempts to search the cottage in which he lived, and what did the people responsible hope to find? He thought of them in the plural because a glance at the havoc wrought convinced him that no single pair of hands could have been responsible for it in the time. There had been at least two, possibly more than two, people at the cottage during the time Smillit had met his death, and one of those two had been a woman.

The footmark had been made after the rain had fallen, which meant that its owner had been there after twenty-past two if the doctor's assertion was to be relied on. And the doctor had recognised the handkerchief he had found, and not only recognised it but its presence had alarmed him. Mr. Budd had made no comment concerning the expression of alarm and that rapid changing of colour, which had accompanied the sight of the handkerchief in his hand. But he had noted it and wondered, and was still wondering.

He sat on the edge of his bed smoking thoughtfully, his sleepy eyes gazing dreamily through the open casement at the roses in Mr. Mutch's back garden. There was no reason at all why he should worry himself over the matter. The most sensible thing to do would be to leave it to Sergeant Buckle and the rather overbearing McNeill. It was their job, let them get on with it. Why should he spoil the last week of his holiday by worrying about mysterious women and half-remembered phrases.

It was queer how that kept coming back to his mind. 'The whispering pines'. Why should that strike him as being familiar? He frowned, made an impatient gesture, and rising to his feet went downstairs to seek out old Jacob and renew the discussion on black spot and mould which bedtime had interrupted on the previous night, determined to put completely out of his head all thought of the mystery attaching to Bob Smillit's murder.

He was not altogether successful. The crime and its peculiar circumstances kept intruding into his thoughts, and even his interest in roses and everything appertaining to their growth and well-being failed to keep it out.

It was not, however, until late evening that any fresh development occurred, and then Mr. Budd was destined to receive the surprise of his life. It was a practice with Jacob Mutch to walk over to the Avernly Arms and fetch the supper beer. Now and again, when he was staying there, Mr. Budd would accompany him and they would have a drink before returning to the evening meal. On this occasion Mr. Mutch went alone, leaving his friend and lodger enjoying the beauties of the garden.

Usually old Jacob was gone about half an hour on these expeditions but this evening he was back in under fifteen minutes, rather breathless and with his lined face full of excitement.

' 'Ere, Mr. B.,' he panted, speaking with difficulty in his anxiety to recount his news, 'there's a feller over at the Arms wot looks suspicious. Everybody's talkin' about 'im!'

Mr. Budd removed his nose from a deep red bloom, which he had been sniffing appreciatively.

'How d'you mean he looks suspicious?' he inquired.

'Well, 'e's a stranger in these parts,' said

old Jacob. 'A tall chap with a black beard which anyone could tell ain't real. Been in the bar most of the evenin', 'e 'as, drinkin' lime juice!' He offered this last piece of information disgustedly as if it was sufficient indication of the bearded stranger's bad character.

'Wearin' a false beard, is he,' said Mr. Budd, rubbing his chin. 'Sounds queer. I'll come and have a look at him.'

'I thought you might like to,' said Mr. Mutch, 'that's why I 'urried back and told you.'

The Avernly Arms was barely a hundred and fifty yards up the street, an old-fashioned inn with windows on either side of the narrow entrance. Mr. Budd and his companion entered the bar and pushing their way through the crowd reached the counter.

'There ye are!' said Mr. Mutch. 'That's the feller, look!' He nodded towards a man who was standing alone, staring gloomily at a half empty glass in front of him. A cap was drawn down over his eyes and the lower part of his face was almost entirely concealed beneath a bushy black

40

beard that was so palpably false that Mr. Budd stared in amazement as he saw it.

'So that's him, is it?' he murmured, and then his jaw dropped. 'Good Lord!' he gasped, and to the astonishment of Mr. Mutch and the rest of the frequenters of the Avernly Arms he pushed his way towards the stranger and tapped him on the arm. 'Come outside!' he said.

The bearded man followed him without a word, and in the twilight of the Summer evening Mr. Budd faced him.

'Now, Leek,' he said, 'perhaps you'll tell me what the dickens you're playin' at, wanderin' about the country got up like a stage detective!'

4

Sergeant Leek explains

' 'Ow did you spot me?' asked Sergeant Leek mournfully.

'How did I spot you!' repeated Mr. Budd. 'How did I spot you! D'you seriously think that thing is a disguise. What is it? An old hearth-rug?'

'No, it's a proper beard,' said Leek. 'I used it once at Christmas, in amachure theatricals, when I was playin' Macbeth.'

The stout Superintendent swallowed with difficulty.

'Are you tryin' to pass yourself off as Macbeth now?' he demanded sarcastically. 'D'you know there isn't a policeman who wouldn't arrest you on sight. Even a child of six could tell that wasn't a real beard.'

'I didn't think it looked so bad,' protested the unfortunate sergeant, 'and I didn't want to be spotted.'

'I see,' broke in Mr. Budd. 'Well, what's the idea? What are you doin' here?'

'Well, you see it's like this,' explained Leek, a little aggrievedly. 'I was told to keep an eye on Harry Milton, you know — '

'I know Harry Milton,' interrupted Mr. Budd impatiently, 'the 'peterman'.'

'That's right,' went on Leek. 'We got news at the Yard that 'Arry was contemplatin' a bust, and I was put on to shadder 'im. Well, 'e knows me pretty well and as I didn't want to be recognised I thought I'd just alter my appearance a bit so as not to attract attention — '

'I see,' grunted Mr. Budd. 'You didn't think of engaging a band or hirin' a horse and pretendin' to be Lady Godiva? I should think either would have attracted less attention than your present get-up. Is Harry down here?'

Leek shook his head gloomily.

'I don't know where 'e is,' he confessed. 'I lost 'im last night. But knowin' 'e'd taken a ticket 'ere I thought if I 'ung about I might pick 'im up again.'

Mr. Budd screwed up his face thoughtfully. Harry Milton was a well-known safe breaker. He specialised in banks. It was unlikely that anything so small as Pine Cottage would attract his attention, but he had been in the vicinity and Mr. Budd was convinced that there was something very big behind Smillit's murder. And if there was, it was more than possible that Milton was in it. He was one of the cleverest safe breakers in England; had worked with some of the big men; was believed, although this had never been proved, to have been the right hand of Joe Rennett.

'Did you know there'd been a murder committed last night?' he asked.

The sergeant nodded.

'Yes,' he replied. 'They was talkin' about it inside.' He jerked his head towards the inn. 'That's why I was stayin' on, I wanted to 'ear more.'

Mr. Budd pinched his upper lip and considered.

'Wait here,' he ordered. 'Take that piece of nonsense off your face and I'll join you in a minute.'

He returned to the bar, and under the curious gaze of the habitués sought out old Jacob Mutch. The old man was consuming the dregs of a pint of beer.

'I'm bringin' that feller back to your cottage, if you don't mind, Jacob,' whispered the stout Superintendent. 'He's one of our men. I believe he's got some information that may be valuable in the Smillit business.'

Mr. Mutch set down his empty tankard and drew the back of his hand across his lips.

'Anythin' you say, Mr. B., is all right with me,' he declared, and followed the big man outside.

When they rejoined Leek the offending black beard had disappeared and the sergeant was his lugubrious self once more.

'That's better,' said Mr. Budd critically. 'You look less like the wild man from Borneo.'

The sergeant said nothing, but it was obvious from his expression that he was a little aggrieved.

'Now,' continued his superior, as they walked towards the cottage, 'let's hear more about this. You was followin' Harry

Milton and you lost him, is that it?'

'That's right,' answered Leek, and launched into a slightly defensive explanation. It appeared that one Steve Hutch, a 'nose', had notified the Yard that Harry Milton was contemplating a bust, and as he was only out on ticket, having just finished a sentence of eighteen months, Chief Inspector Handcox had sent Leek to pick him up and trail him.

'Did Handcox suggest the inverted busby?' interrupted Mr. Budd, and Leek shook his head.

'No,' he replied. 'That was me own idea.'

'I guessed as much,' growled the big man. 'Go on.'

Leek had trailed Harry about most of the day, and had succeeded in getting sufficiently close to him at Waterloo to hear him book to Avernly. He had taken a ticket too, but at the station had mislaid it, and by the time he had found it his quarry had disappeared.

'I was 'opin' I'd be able to pick 'im up again,' concluded the sergeant mournfully.

'Do you mean to say,' demanded Mr.

Budd, 'that you was trailin' him about London wearin' that bird's nest?'

The sergeant shook his head.

'No,' he replied, 'I put that on in the train. You see I thought that if 'e'd spotted me durin' the day 'e wouldn't recognise me in me disguise.'

'H'm!' grunted the Superintendent. 'Well, I suppose you know that the whole village is under the impression that you're the murderer of this feller Smillit? And judgin' from your appearance when I saw you in the bar you can't blame 'em. Gosh!' Words failed him.

They had reached the gate of the cottage and were on the point of turning in when Mr. Budd saw, out of the corner of his eye, two people who were standing under a clump of trees a few yards away. In spite of the blue dusk of the summer evening he recognised the pair. One was the girl, Olivia Brade, whom he had seen that morning, and the other was Doctor Carr. They were talking earnestly and the doctor must have said something about the big man, for the girl turned round quickly, and as quickly looked away again.

Mr. Budd frowned as he walked ponderously up the little paved path to the porch. The doctor had recognised that handkerchief which he had found in the garden of Smillit's cottage, and now he was talking to Olivia Brade. Was there any connection? If there was there could only be one. The girl had been the owner of that handkerchief, and it had been her foot which had left the print in the wet earth of the flowerbed.

In spite of the fact that he was on holiday and that really the affair was nothing to do with him, he found it impossible not to be interested. His long training and the very genuine love which he had for his profession forced him to try and seek a solution almost against his inclination.

It was a curious business, and the introduction of Harry Milton made it no less curious. What had brought that expert safebreaker and bank smasher to Avernly? Was it purely a coincidence or was he, in some inexplicable way, mixed up with the murder? He couldn't have been responsible for it, for at the time it was committed he was in London and under the observation of Leek. But that didn't say that he didn't know something about it.

During supper and after he was a silent and thoughtful man. Leek's original intention had been to try and fix up a room at the Avernly Arms, and but for the Superintendent's intervention he would have carried out this project. There was a tiny apartment, however, little more than a box room, which Mrs. Mutch hospitably placed at his disposal.

They went to bed early. The Mutches seldom stayed up after ten, and Mr. Budd, when he was a member of the household, conformed to this rule, too, and was glad of the unaccustomed luxury, for during his normal life he was awake at all hours of the night.

The village sensation occupied his mind for a little while after he had blown out his candle and settled down to rest, and he could not have stated accurately when conscious thought merged into dreams. At one moment he was speculating upon the reason for Harry Milton's presence in the neighbourhood, and the next he was strapped to a board while Sergeant Leek, with a fiendish expression on his long, melancholy face, was throwing knives which thudded all around him.

He awoke with a start, the thudding still in his ears, and discovered that it came from downstairs, and emanated from an impatient hand that was wielding the knocker on the front door.

As he sat up in bed, blinking the sleep from his eyes, he heard a window go up and the voice of Mr. Mutch enquiring angrily what the adjectival row was about. A rather incoherent and throaty voice answered him.

'I want to see the gentleman wot's stayin' with yer. It's a policeman, ain't 'e?'

'Oh, it's you, Jim Bates, is it?' growled Mr. Mutch. 'Wot the 'ell d'you want to come knockin' respectable people up at this hour for?'

'I want to speak to the Superintendent,' retorted Mr. Bates. 'There's a dead 'un in Thorn Lane . . .'

Mr. Budd was out of bed and over to the window before Mr. Mutch's reply came. Leaning out he saw, in the light of dawn, a roughly clad man standing in the little front garden.

'What is it?' he demanded. 'I'm Superintendent Budd.'

The labourer touched his cap.

'There's a dead man in Thorn Lane, sir,' he answered shakily. 'I just found 'im, and as there ain't no police station nearer than Sellington I thought I'd better come 'ere.'

'You did quite right,' grunted the stout Superintendent. 'Wait a minute while I get some clothes on.'

He dressed hurriedly and went downstairs. Mr. Mutch, clad in an old coat, was standing at the open front door, his face working with excitement.

'Go and wake Sergeant Leek,' said Mr. Budd, but there was no need, for at that moment the sergeant appeared, an inelegant figure in a pair of trousers and pyjama jacket, his dishevelled hair sticking out oddly from his thin head.

'What's up?' he asked sleepily.

'We're all up,' snarled Mr. Budd. 'Go and put your coat on.' He turned to the excited Mr. Bates. 'Now then, what's all this about a dead man?' he demanded, and the labourer was only too eager to tell the story.

He had been on his way to work and was taking a short cut through Thorn Lane when he had seen a man lying under a hedge near Smillit's cottage. Thinking at first he was a tramp asleep he was passing without taking much notice when he had seen blood staining the grass on which he lay. A closer investigation had revealed a wound in the man's forehead and the fact that he was dead.

By the time he had disjointedly finished his tale Leek appeared, more respectably clad.

'You'd better come with us,' said Mr. Budd, and Jim Bates, whose first horror had been replaced by one of curiosity and a feeling of importance, assented.

They walked quickly along the deserted street, a strange looking trio, for both the sergeant and Mr. Budd were dressed sketchily. Reaching the entrance to Thorn Lane Jim Bates slowed and pointed to a sprawling thing that lay in the shadow of a hedge, on the opposite side to Smillit's cottage.

'There y'are,' he said hoarsely.

Mr. Budd and the sergeant went over, and the big man peered down. The dead man lay on his back, one arm flung out, the other doubled up under him. His eyes were half closed, and in the centre of his forehead was a bluish-red circle, from which the blood had trickled down the side of his face to spread in an irregular pool on the grass where his head rested.

As Mr. Budd looked at him the breath came hissing through his teeth. The man was Harry Milton, and he had been shot at close quarters, for the powder marks were clearly visible round the wound in his forehead.

5

The owner of the cottage

He confirmed the identity of the dead man with Leek, although this was unnecessary. He had known the bank robber sufficiently well to recognize him at first glance.

'Where's the nearest telephone?' he asked, looking up at the curious and interested Mr. Bates.

The labourer scratched his head.

'The Avernly Arms 'ud be the nearest,' he replied, 'but they're still abed — '

'Go and knock 'em up!' ordered the stout Superindent, turning to Leek. 'Get on to the police station at Sellington and notify Sergeant Buckle of what's occurred. Tell him we've identified the man, and it's murder.'

'Why d'you think — ' began the sergeant, but his superior interrupted him.

'We haven't got time to hold a debate!' he snapped. 'Go and do as you're told.'

Leek moved off, and Mr. Budd, caressing his chins, looked down at the body.

'You didn't touch him at all?' he asked, and Jim shook his head.

'No sir,' he answered. 'I didn't go near enough. I jest saw 'e was a dead 'un and ran as quick as I could to Mutch's cottage. Who d'you think can 'ave done it, sir? The same feller wot did in Bob Smillit?'

'Most likely,' murmured Mr. Budd, absently. 'You'd better stop here, Bates. Sergeant Buckle 'ull want to see you when he arrives.'

Mr. Bates made no demur. He had evidently had every intention of stopping. It was not often that such a sensation interrupted the normal course of his uneventful life, and he wasn't, if he could help it, going to miss a second of his enjoyment. What a story he would have to recount to his cronies in the bar of the Avernly Arms that night, and for many nights to come. In his mind's eye he could visualize just how important he would become, and his chest expanded.

'If there's anythin' I can do to help, sir, I'll be only too willin',' he said.

Mr. Budd nodded. His sleepy eyes were searching the ground in the vicinity of the body. The grass was short and uneven and had retained no impression. One thing was certain, there had been no struggle. If there had it couldn't have failed to have left visible marks, and there were none.

The man had been dead for some time. The blood on his face was dry, as also was the stain on the grass beneath his head. A thought struck him, and he looked towards the cottage. Surely Superintendent McNeill had arranged to leave a constable on guard, or hadn't he? Apparently he hadn't, for if there had been anyone there they could scarcely have failed to hear the shot. And yet it was peculiar. It was hardly likely that the premises in which a murder had been committed would have been left without someone in charge.

'Stop here,' he said to Mr. Bates. 'Don't

touch nothin', and see that no one comes near. I'll be back in a minute.'

He walked ponderously across to the little gate, pushed it open, and made his way up the path. There was no sign of life but when he reached the door he saw that it was ajar. His brows drew together as he pushed it open and peered into the darkness of the passageway beyond.

'Anyone there?' he called sharply, but only the echo of his voice answered him.

Although fairly light outside the interior of the cottage was gloomy and he could see little. Crossing the threshold he advanced slowly along the passage until he came to a door that gave admittance to the tiny kitchen. This was only half closed, and throwing it open to he looked into the little room beyond.

The morning light filtered greyly through the unshuttered window, and the first thing he saw was the burly form of the bucolic policeman who had accompanied Buckle that morning doubled up on the floor beside the table.

Going quickly over he knelt down. The man was still breathing. On the back of his head was a contused lump.

'Coshed!' murmured Mr. Budd softly. 'And people talk about comin' to the country for peace and quiet! H'm!'

He rose to his feet with difficulty, went out into the little scullery, found a towel and soaking it at the sink came back and bathed the constable's head and face, After a little while the man opened his eyes.

'Keep still,' warned Mr. Budd, as he moved easily. 'You've had a nasty crack and you won't feel well for a bit.'

The constable groaned and stared up at him.

'What 'appened?' he murmured. 'Gosh! My 'ead don't 'alf ache!'

'You're lucky to be able to feel anythin',' grunted the stout Superintendent, and taking off his coat rolled it into an improvised cushion, which he slipped beneath the other's injured head. 'Just you keep quiet and you'll be all right.'

'Somethin' 'it me — ' began the constable, and Mr. Budd nodded.

'Yes, I think it did,' he answered. 'Don't talk. You can make a statement later.'

He began an inspection of the ground floor of the cottage. The room in which Smillit had been killed was untouched since he had seen it last, except that the body of that unfortunate man had been removed. He found nothing of interest downstairs and ascended to the bedrooms.

Here everything was also the same as it had been on the previous day. McNeill had evidently issued instructions that the place was to be left exactly as it had been found when the murder of Smillit had been discovered. This was only natural, and the big man had expected nothing else. There was no clue to the intruder who had bludgeoned the constable and he completed his search no wiser than he had been when he started.

The man was sitting up when he came back to the kitchen, rubbing his head tenderly.

'Feelin' better?' asked Mr. Budd kindly, and the constable nodded a little dazedly.

'Yes, sir,' he answered, 'I feel horribly sick . . . '

'That'll go off,' said the big man

encouragingly. 'How did this happen?'

The man looked at him dully.

'Well, I don't rightly know, sir,' he replied. 'I was sittin' 'ere in the kitchen thinkin' about makin' a cup of tea when somebody knocked at the door — the front door. I went to see who it was and there weren't no one there. I knew I couldn't 'ave been mistaken, and I thought p'raps whoever it was might 'ave stepped to one side like. I went out to see and that's all I remember.'

Mr. Budd pulled at his fleshy nose and grunted.

'You didn't see anyone?' he inquired.

'No, sir,' answered the constable. 'I didn't see nothin'. Somethin' 'it me a whacking smack on the 'ead and I don't remember nothin' more until I found you stoopin' over me.'

The big man pursed his lips.

'What time did this happen?' he inquired.

'It was just beginnin' to get light,' said the man. 'Not really dawn, if you know what I mean, sir, but a sort of a greyish look in the sky.'

'H'm!' commented the Superintendent. 'Well, you'd better sit over there and take it easy. When the doctor comes I'll get him to have a look at you.'

'The doctor?' said the policeman in a puzzled voice, and Mr. Budd nodded.

'Yes,' he answered briefly. 'There was another murder committed here last night. A fellow called Harry Milton, a well-known thief, was shot dead out in the lane.'

The constable gaped at him.

'Blimey!' he breathed. 'The feller who shot him must have been the chap who coshed me.'

'Maybe,' said the stout Superintendent non-committally and helped the injured man to his feet. 'Now, you sit over there,' he said again. 'I've notified Sergeant Buckle, and when he arrives you can repeat your story to him.'

He put on his coat, left the bewildered policeman nursing his injured head, and went back to Jim Bates. As he joined him Leek's thin figure appeared at the end of the lane.

'I've been on to the station,' said the

sergeant breathlessly, when he came up to them, 'and they're getting in touch with Buckle. He's at home and in bed, so the feller on duty told me, but it won't take long to dig him out. 'E ought to be 'ere soon.'

'That's fine,' said Mr. Budd. 'The policeman on duty over at the cottage,' — he jerked his head in the direction of the little gate — 'has had a nasty crack. Go over and keep him company, will you?'

'What d'you mean?' asked Leek, with wide eyes. 'Been coshed, 'as he?'

'If you prefer that!' snapped his superior. 'Can't you ever do anythin' without makin' a song and dance about it?'

'Well, I was only — ' protested the injured Leek,

'You're always 'only' doin' somethin',' growled Mr. Budd. 'Go and do what I tell you and don't argue.'

Leek gave a resigned sigh and went immediately. The big man hesitated for a moment and then stooping over the body began a quick search of the clothing.

Strictly speaking he was going beyond his rights. The crime had been committed outside the Metropolitan area, and unless the Chief Constable of the County invited his cooperation he had no right to interfere. But ethics had never worried him much, and he was too interested to bother now.

In the outside pocket of the overcoat that Milton was wearing he discovered a short, thick, rubber cosh. It was specked with blood to which several hairs were adhering. There was little doubt that this was the weapon that had struck the policeman down, and it suggested that the hand that had wielded it had been the dead man's. This was by no means certain since the murderer might quite easily have slipped it into Milton's pocket after he had shot him. It was a possibility worth considering, however, and Mr. Budd made a mental note.

The rest of his search drew a blank. There was a cigarette case partly filled with a cheap brand of Virginia cigarettes, a small amount of money in silver in one of the trouser pockets, and two notes for a

pound each in the upper left hand pocket
of the waistcoat. That was all.

He straightened up, red faced and breathing heavily from his task, and looked at
the interested Mr. Bates.

'How long have you lived in this
district?' he asked.

'Me?' said the labourer. 'I was born
'ere.'

'Then you know most of the people?'
continued the stout Superintendent.
'How long has Doctor Carr been here?'

Jim Bates considered.

'Nearly four year,' he replied after a
pause.

'Four years, eh?' said Mr. Budd. 'And
what about Miss Brade?'

'Oh, she ain't been 'ere very long,' said
the man. 'Not more than seven or eight
months.'

'Who is she?' asked Mr. Budd, putting
the same question he had put to the bank
manager.

'Well, she's a lady,' replied Jim Bates
hesitantly. 'I dunno as I can tell you much
more about 'er, sir. She lives in a little
cottage t'other side of the village, up by

the green. Holly 'Ouse, it's called. This is a queer business, ain't it?' he went on conversationally. 'First poor old Bob Smillit, now this 'ere feller, and old Whittle biffed on the 'ead.'

'Yes, it's a very queer business,' said Mr. Budd thoughtfully. 'Very queer indeed. How long have you been comin' this way to go to your work?'

'Matter o' ten year,' said Mr. Bates rather surprised at the question.

'I see.' The Superintendent pinched a fold of flesh at his neck. 'And you've always been in the habit of passin' the cottage?'

'That's right, sir. I turns off over that little stile there and across the field. Saves me a tidy bit it do.'

'I daresay.' The lids had drooped over the big man's eyes. He was staring beyond Mr. Bates at some imaginary object in mid-air. 'D'you remember the fellow who had this place before Smillit?'

'Middle-aged feller you mean,' said Mr. Bates promptly. 'Chap wot only spent part of 'is time down 'ere. Used to come on a Friday and leave on a Monday.'

'That's the man,' agreed Mr. Budd. 'He

went away suddenly, didn't he?'

'Yes, sir. We wondered in the village wot 'ad 'appened to 'im,' said the labourer. 'Funny sort of chap. Never said nothin' much to no one. Used to go scorching about on a motorbike.'

Mr. Budd's eyes opened suddenly very wide.

'On a motorbike, eh?' he said softly, and into his mind came the phrase which had bothered him so during the preceding day: 'With the breeze whispering through the pines.'

For no reason at all it had suddenly occurred to him where he had heard those words before. In his mind's eye he saw a comfortably furnished flat and a middle-aged man with horn-rimmed glasses smiling blandly. 'You'll never catch me, Budd,' he was saying. 'Not in a thousand years. Long before then I shall have retired to some little place in the country where I can hear the breeze whispering through the pines.'

Vividly the picture came to him. He could almost hear the slightly husky voice —

66

'This motorbike you're talkin' about, was it a big, red, Silbeam?' he asked abruptly.

'That's right, sir,' said Mr. Bates, whose hobby was tinkering with motorcycles. 'A beauty she were too.'

Mr. Budd fetched a long sigh. There was little doubt in his mind now who the man was who had come down for weekends to Pine Cottage and suddenly hadn't come any more. It was Joe Rennett.

6

Five hundred thousand dollars

Sergeant Buckle arrived a few minutes later, a surprised and rather bewildered man, for such sensational happenings had never before occurred within his orbit.

Mr. Budd acquainted him with all he knew, omitting, however, all mention of Joe Rennett and, leaving him in charge, collected Leek and returned to Mr. Mutch's cottage.

He was a silent and thoughtful man on the way back, and Leek, who from long association knew something of his moods, refrained from putting the question that hovered on his tongue. Mr. and Mrs. Mutch, however, were not so reticent. Habitual laziness had prevented the old man from dressing and accompanying them, and now that they had returned they were met with a flood of eager demands to know what had happened.

The big man satisfied their curiosity as briefly as possible during breakfast, and when the meal was over carted the sergeant up to his room.

'Now listen here,' he said, 'I don't know what you were goin' to do this mornin', whether you were goin' back to the Yard or whether you were goin' on chasin' up Harry Milton. However, whatever you were goin' to do is all altered now.'

'I'll 'ave to report what's 'appened,' put in Leek.

'You won't have to do anythin' of the sort,' retorted Mr. Budd. 'I'm gettin' on to the Assistant Commissioner myself.'

The sergeant's rather fish-like eyes opened to their widest extent.

'You are?' he said.

'Yes, I am!' replied his superior. 'That is, of course,' he added, 'unless you've got any objections?'

'No, why should I 'ave?' said Leek seriously.

'I only just wanted to know,' said Mr. Budd. 'If you'd have objected of course it would have put me in a difficult position. Naturally I wouldn't like to go against your personal feelin's. There's a big thing behind this.' His voice changed suddenly and he became serious. 'A very big thing!'

'I don't see anythin' in a little crook like Milton bein' bumped off,' said the sergeant.

'I'm not talkin' about Milton bein' bumped off,' said the stout Superintendent. 'I'm talkin' about five hundred thousand dollars. You show me somethin' bigger than that and I'll be pleased to see it.'

Leek gasped.

'Five hundred thousand dollars?' he repeated. 'What d'you mean?'

'That was the sum,' explained Mr. Budd carefully, 'that Joe Rennett took from the American Exchange Bank of New York on a Sunday mornin' just under a year ago.'

'I remember that case,' said the sergeant, nodding. 'But what's that got to do with Harry Milton and this other murder? Rennet's dead. He died in a motor accident.'

'I know he's dead,' replied the big man. 'And I know he died in a motor accident.

But that five hundred thousand dollars didn't die with him: it disappeared, and nobody's been able to find it.'

A light of understanding came into Leek's eyes,

'D'you mean to say,' he gasped, 'that Harry Milton was after that money?'

'That I don't know,' said Mr. Budd, pursing his lips and gently rubbing the lowest of his many chins. 'But somebody's after it. I'm pretty sure in my own mind that that money's at the bottom of all that's been happenin' round here.'

'Why?' demanded the sergeant, not unreasonably.

'Because,' explained his superior, 'the fellow who had that cottage before Smillit was Joe Rennett.'

'How d'you know that?' inquired Leek.

'Never mind how I know it!' snapped the big man impatiently. 'I do know it, and that's sufficient. I was in charge of that American bank affair, and the fact that the money was never found didn't altogether put me in the good books of the 'people upstairs' — he always referred to the Administrative of Scotland Yard as

71

the 'people upstairs' — 'So,' he went on, 'if there's any chance of recovering that money I'm on it. Now do you understand?'

Leek nodded slowly.

'Yes,' he answered. 'And I suppose you want me to stay down 'ere and 'elp?'

'I want you to stay down here,' corrected Mr. Budd. 'That feller from Readin', a bony piece of work called McNeill, is so full of his own importance that I'm goin' to have difficulty. But maybe if I get on the right side of Colonel Blair he'll be able to do somethin', particularly if I hint to him that there's a possibility of recoverin' this money.'

Leek's mind had been working, and now he put into words the result of his silent cogitation.

'What I can't understand,' he said slowly, 'is, if somebody's after this five 'undred thousand why they've left it so long. It's a good time now since Rennett was killed. If anyone knew where the stuff was 'id why didn't they go after it at once?'

'If I could tell you that I could tell you

a lot more,' said Mr. Budd. 'There's just a possibility that the person behind these two killin's has only just learned where the money is. Smillit's cottage was burgled twice before he was murdered. I don't know if you knew that, but anyway, you know it now. And nothin' was took! Does that suggest anythin'?'

The sergeant screwed up his face.

'You mean they was after some clue concernin' the whereabouts of the stuff?' he said hesitantly, and brightened considerably when the big man nodded.

'You're scintillatin' this mornin',' he said. 'Must be the air of this place clearin' the cobwebs out of your brain. Yes, that's exactly what I do mean. The person or persons who broke into Smillit's cottage were lookin' for some clue to where Rennett had hidden the proceeds of his last robbery.'

'It couldn't 'ave been Milton,' declared Leek. 'He's only been out o' prison a week.'

'I know that,' said Mr. Budd. 'I know it wasn't Milton. I also know it wasn't Milton who killed Smillit. But it was the person who killed Milton and Smillit, and he's the person we've got to find.'

'It don't look as if it's goin' to be too easy to me,' remarked Leek, a dubious expression on his long face.

'I didn't expect it 'ud be simple,' said the Superintendent. 'Nothin' that's worth doin' is easy. Now, you wait there. I'm goin' along to the Post Office to put a call through to the Yard. You can occupy your time thinkin' over what I've told you, and if anythin' suggests itself to you let me know.'

He left the lean sergeant sitting on the edge of the bed, his face contorted into a painful expression of concentration.

The Post Office lay at the foot of the little High Street, and as he turned into its narrow door he saw Olivia Brade buying stamps from the counter, and she gave him a half nod as she hurriedly collected her change and went out.

While he waited for his call to be put through he tried to fit this girl into his theory concerning Rennett and the missing money. What had she to do with it, and what had taken her to Smillit's cottage at such a peculiar hour on the morning he had met his death?

He was connected with the Yard before any satisfactory answer to this question occurred to him. For nearly twenty minutes, with the door of the cabinet tight shut, he talked with the Assistant Commissioner, and by the time he emerged, perspiring but cheerful, he had gained his point.

That afternoon there arrived at the door of Mr. Mutch's humble cottage an imposing and glittering saloon, out of which stepped a thin, grey-haired man, whose tanned cheeks and military bearing proclaimed the retired army officer which he was.

Mr. Budd interviewed him alone in the tiny parlour,

'I'm Colonel Hothling,' he introduced himself, and the big man nodded.

'I've been expecting you, sir,' he murmured.

'I've had a request from the Yard which is a little peculiar,' went on the Colonel, eyeing the stout, sleepy-eyed man before him in faint surprise. 'I have been asked to afford you every facility in investigating the two murders which have been committed in this district within the last forty-eight hours. And although, as you are aware, Scotland Yard does not, as a rule, interfere outside its own — er'

'Area,' suggested Mr. Budd helpfully.

'Boundary,' corrected Colonel Hothling, a little stiffly. 'As I was saying, although Scotland Yard does not interfere beyond its own boundary — that of the Metropolitan District — I have acceded to the request.'

'Thank you, sir,' murmured the Superintendent.

'I have instructed McNeill, one of my most able men, by the way,' continued the Chief Constable, 'to give you every help and assistance that lies in his power. He was — er — naturally, a little — er — shall we say disgruntled, but I assured him that in the circumstances no doubt was being cast on his ability, but that peculiar reasons made it necessary that you should be more or less in charge of the case.'

He paused, and since he obviously

expected it Mr. Budd said. 'Thank you, sir,' again.

'I must confess,' remarked the Colonel, 'that but for this — er — request of the Assistant Commissioner's I should not have called in outside assistance. I rather think that I and my men are capable of dealing with any ordinary crime that may be committed within our jurisdiction.' He drew himself up unconsciously as he spoke and his chest expanded several inches.

The stout Superintendent was waiting for him to drag in a remark about his brigade and Poona, but if the Colonel had any such intention he thought better of it. It was the big man who broke the rather awkward silence that followed.

'I'm much obliged to you, Colonel Hothling,' he said. 'And I shall be only too happy to work with Superintendent McNeill. The only reason for the interference of the Yard is that, in my opinion, these murders have their beginnings in an old case on which I was engaged and which was never brought to a satisfactory conclusion.'

'So I'm given to understand,' said the Colonel. 'Connected with Joe Rennett and the robbery of the American Bank, wasn't it?'

'That's right, sir,' said Mr. Budd, nodding.

'I remember reading about it,' remarked the Chief Constable. 'Interesting business. Something like five hundred thousand dollars were involved I believe.'

'Which was never found,' said the big man.

'And you believe that money's at the bottom of these two murders?' inquired the Colonel.

'I do, sir,' said Mr. Budd. 'I believe that money is hidden somewhere, and not very far away from where we are at the moment. And I'm goin' to find it.'

'Well, you can count on us,' said the Colonel. 'We'll give you every assistance, Superintendent, every assistance!'

7

Leek has an idea

Mr. Budd spent a busy afternoon. His holiday had come to an untimely end, and although he was disappointed that his peace should have been so rudely broken into he was compensated to a large extent by the possibility of being able to finish a job which had been left more or less in the air.

He returned with the Chief Constable to Reading and had a long conference with Superintendent McNeill. That frigid man greeted him coldly and obviously regarded him as an interloper. This worried the stout Superintendent not at all, since whatever McNeill's feelings might be he couldn't very well do anything else in the circumstances but proffer such assistance as he was able.

Rather to his surprise Mr. Budd seemed interested in only two things, or, to be more exact, two persons, Doctor Carr and Olivia Brade. McNeill was forced to admit that he knew very little about either. Carr had come to Avernly just under four years previously. He was the police doctor for Avernly and Sellington, and such duties as fell to him he carried out conscientiously. That was all the Superintendent knew about him. Concerning Olivia Brade he was even more vague. He suggested that Mr. Budd would probably get more information from Sergeant Buckle, but in this he was wrong, for when the big man interviewed Buckle later that worthy could tell him very little.

'She just came 'ere and took 'Olly 'Ouse, but I don't know nothin' about her, sir,' said the sergeant rather apologetically. 'You see I never 'ad no call to inquire about a lady like that. There's quite a lot of people in Avernly that I don't know much about.'

'Yes, of course, that's natural,' said Mr. Budd. 'I'd like to know somethin' about this girl, though, because I'm pretty sure it was she who was in Smillit's garden that night.'

Buckle's eyes expanded until they threatened to out of his head.

'Miss Brade?' he exclaimed.

Budd nodded.

'Yes. You needn't go repeatin' that to your Superintendent,' he remarked. 'I haven't told him why I'm makin' inquiries about her.'

A slow grin appeared on the red face of the sergeant.

'All right, sir,' he answered. 'I'm not given to gossip. And Superintendent McNeill is a bit difficult now and again.

'Mostly now!' grunted Mr. Budd, for he disliked that raw-boned official intensely. 'If I'd told him he'd have had her under arrest in an hour. That feller's got one idea of investigatin' a crime, and that's to lock everybody up and so make sure he doesn't miss the right one.'

This slanderous statement was based on an element of truth, for he had had great difficulty in dissuading McNeill from issuing a warrant for the arrest of the unfortunate Jim Bates.

Dusk was falling when he came back to the cottage and discovered Leek awaiting him anxiously.

'I've got an idea,' said the lean sergeant,

81

when they were closeted alone. 'It came to me sudden-like this afternoon.'

'Let's hear it,' grunted Mr. Budd.

'Supposin',' said Leek, 'this feller Joe Rennett ain't dead after all.'

'Eh!' Mr. Budd sat up suddenly. 'What d'you mean, ain't dead? He's been buried for nearly twelve months!'

'Somebody's been buried,' agreed Leek, 'but was it Joe Rennett? If you remember he was so badly messed about that identification was difficult. You and me went down to the mortuary. Now, if he ain't dead that 'ud explain things, wouldn't it?'

'It would explain some things,' said his superior. 'I wonder if you've really hit on somethin' sensible for the first time in your life!'

'Those things come to me in flashes,' said Leek complacently. 'I can't account for it. They just come into me mind without me knowing it. When I was a boy — '

'I don't want your autobiography,' said Mr. Budd. 'If this idea of yours leads anywhere it'll be the first you've ever had in your life, and I'll see that you get some suitable recognition. But in the meantime don't go gettin' a swollen head. It's only an idea, remember.'

'But it fits all the facts,' argued Leek, anxious to impress his superior with his acumen. 'If Rennett didn't die in that smash then he's the feller we're lookin' for. Most likely he's been lyin' low until all danger of connecting him with the cottage was over.'

Mr. Budd nodded in silence.

'Most likely,' continued the sergeant, enlarging on his original theory, 'he was waitin' for Harry Milton to come out o' prison. Most likely they was in it together.'

'Don't you go lettin' your imagination run away with you,' warned the big man. 'You've struck an idea, and for the moment be content with that. I don't think Harry Milton was in this with anybody. I think he came here on his own, and the other fellow surprised him and killed him.'

'You mean Joe Rennett,' said Leek, and Mr. Budd clicked his teeth impatiently.

'I don't mean nobody!' he snapped. 'We've got no proof that Joe Rennet's alive. I keep on tellin' you it's only an idea of yours, which means that it's probably wrong. However, I'll set inquiries goin' along those lines. Now go and amuse yourself for an hour or two, I want to think.'

The sergeant, his spirits a little dampened, departed mournfully, and Mr. Budd, opening his suitcase, took out a box of his long, black cigars, put them on the table near the bed, and throwing himself down lay staring at the ceiling. After a moment or two he shifted his position, punched the pillows so that they formed a more comfortable rest for his head, lit one of his cigars, and smoked thoughtfully.

There might be something in Leek's suggestion, on the other hand there might not. What was puzzling him was how the girl came into it. Even this he was only basing on a fleeting expression, which he had seen come into the face of Doctor Carr. Olivia Brade might, quite easily, have nothing to do with it at all, but he was pretty sure that the young doctor had recognised the handkerchief, and the fact that he had later been seen speaking to the girl seemed to indicate that she was probably its owner.

For a long time he lay thinking and smoking, and then rousing himself he washed, went downstairs, and inquired for Leek. Mr. Mutch, who occupied his usual position in the porch, informed him that the sergeant was in the garden, and here Mr. Budd discovered him, lugubriously pulling a daisy to pieces.

'She loves me, she loves me not,' he said, and the lean man started and turned. 'Listen,' said the stout Superintendent. 'I'm goin' up to that cottage to have another search, and you're comin' with me. I don't believe it's been properly examined, and I'm goin' to make sure that there's nothing there that may help us.'

'Are you goin' now?' asked Leek, and the other nodded.

The sun had already set and the sky was a deeper blue as they set off along the road towards Thorn Lane. When they reached the abode of the unfortunate Bob Smillit they discovered another constable on guard. Mr. Budd disclosed his identity and the man grinned.

'That's all right, sir,' he said. 'The Superintendent told me to let you do anythin' you wanted.'

'I'm goin' to make a thorough examination of this place,' said Mr. Budd, and the constable's eyes widened.

'I don't think you'll find anythin', sir,' he remarked. 'Both the Superintendent and Sergeant Buckle have been through the place twice, and they ain't found nothin'.'

'Well, there's no harm in my wastin' a little time if I feel like it,' said Mr. Budd, and began his search.

He started with the ground floor, and with the assistance of Leek made a rigorous and detailed examination of every article of furniture. He opened books, shook cushions, pressed and peered at the seats of chairs, tested the flooring and tapped the walls. But, as the constable had predicted, he found nothing. There was no sign of any secret receptacle in which Joe Rennett could have hidden the stolen property, no clue to tell where the money had been put.

When he had exhausted the ground floor he turned his attention to the rooms above, and here he met with the same result. He was a little disappointed, for he had expected to find something. His theory necessitated that there should be some clue in the cottage to the whereabouts of the missing five hundred thousand dollars. He was convinced that it was this that had been at the bottom of the robberies, which Smillit had complained of. It was possible that the marauders had discovered what they were seeking, that the object for which they had come in search was no longer in the cottage. But he was reluctant to believe this. It didn't fit with the facts. If they had discovered what they wanted they wouldn't have come back a third time and so killed Smillit, who had disturbed them. If they had found the thing they were looking for on that third occasion then why had Milton been killed?

Tired from his exertions he sat down in the kitchen and accepted the constable's suggestion of a cup of tea. The whole thing was a mix-up, and even Leek's suggestion concerning Joe Rennett didn't tend to make matters clearer. For if Joe Rennett was still alive he would have had no necessity to search the cottage. He would have known exactly where to lay his hands on what was wanted.

It looked very much to Mr. Budd, when he considered the matter, that there were three people in this. The people who had searched the cottage and killed Bob Smillit, Harry Milton who had come on a similar errand, for obviously it had been he who had coshed the unfortunate policeman, and the unknown who had shot Milton through the head in Thorn Lane. Was this the explanation? Were there three separate and distinct groups after the same object?

This was possible, but it didn't explain the girl, unless she was working in collusion with one of the groups.

The stout Superintendent sipped the hot, strong, decoction that the constable set before him under the mistaken idea that tea should be black with an unpleasant tang, and tried to make some sort of sense out of the disjointed facts he had in his possession. And he found it difficult. If these people were after the money where was it? Evidently Rennett had not hidden it in the cottage. There was no place in which so much as a mouse could have lain concealed, much less a bulky package which five hundred thousand dollars in paper money would occupy.

He finished his tea and yawned wearily.

'There's nothing more to be done here,' he grunted. 'We may as well be getting back.'

They left the constable to the remainder of his lonely vigil and were passing the Avernly Arms when it occurred to Mr. Budd that possibly some information might be gleaned from a chat with the villagers.

He turned in through the narrow entry, accompanied by the melancholy sergeant, and made his way to the sanded bar, where Leek's appearance had caused such a sensation on the previous night. The place was crowded, and their entrance was greeted with a sudden silence and curious looks. Ordering a tankard of beer for himself and a lime-juice for the abstemious Leek he leaned against the counter and surveyed the mixed gathering around him.

It was not until much later that he realized that the clue he had been searching for had been under his nose all the time, but it was in such a conspicuous position and bore such an innocent appearance that both he and all the other people who had searched Pine Cottage had passed it by.

8

Mr. Larkin talks

Mr. Budd had raised his tankard with the intention of pouring a quantity of its contents down his throat when an under-sized little man entered, pushed his way through the crowd, and rapping on the bar with a coin to attract the landlord's attention, demanded in husky voice 'a double whisky.'

Mr. Budd's sleepy eyes caught sight of him and he started.

'Look who's here,' he murmured to Leek, and the sergeant turned his long face in the direction of his superior's eyes.

'Sid Larkin!' he whispered in astonishment. 'What's 'e doin' 'ere?'

Mr. Budd shook his head.

'Perhaps he'll tell us if we're patient,' he remarked. 'He ain't seen us yet.'

The newcomer had been served with his whisky and gulping it down eagerly.

91

His thin, pale face, with its sliver of ginger moustache, looked drawn and haggard; about his small eyes was a shifty expression, and the none too clean hand that held his glass shook.

'Looks as if he's had a shock,' murmured the stout superintendent. 'Well, maybe he's in for another!'

The man finished his drink and pushed the glass across to be refilled.

The habitués of the bar were regarding him anxiously, as the inhabitants of any village always regard a stranger. But Mr. Larkin took no notice of their curiosity. His thin lips were moving and every now and again a muscle in his left cheek twitched. He was obviously suffering from some form of shock.

The second drink was supplied to him and he swallowed it down as quickly as he had dealt with the first. A tinge of colour came into his pale cheeks and with clumsy fingers he fumbled in a pocket of his waistcoat and produced a cheap packet of cigarettes. Pulling one out he stuck it in his mouth and lit it, inhaling the smoke with the air of one who found its influence soothing.

'Stop here,' murmured Mr. Budd, and began to edge his way ponderously through the group of villagers in his immediate vicinity towards the little man.

He came up beside him without the other being aware of his presence and set his half-filled tankard down on the counter.

'Well, now, this is a surprise,' he said genially. 'Who'd have thought of finding you here!'

Mr. Larkin started violently, turned, and his face went the colour of chalk.

'Blimey,' he breathed, 'it's Budd!'

'What you goin' to have, Sid?' said the stout Superintendent jovially.

'I don't want nothin',' muttered Larkin. 'I'm goin'.' He turned, but Mr. Budd laid a huge hand on his arm.

'Don't be in such a hurry,' he said. 'It's not like you, Sid, to run away from an old friend. Stop and have a little chat.'

The man's eyes regarded him suspiciously.

'I don't want no little chat with you,' he muttered. 'What's the game, eh?'

'There ain't no game that I know of,' answered the big man. 'Surely when a feller meets an old acquaintance in a pub the first thing he does is to ask him to have one. Besides, it's a long time since I've seen you, and I'd like to talk things over.'

'What things?' demanded Mr. Larkin quickly. 'You've got nothin' on me, Budd. I'm runnin' straight now.'

'Sure! Of course you are,' answered the other. 'I've never met a crook yet who wasn't. The remarkable thin' to me is how there's ever any burglaries and such-like with all you fellers runnin' straight. It's often occurred to me who does these crimes.'

Mr. Larkin muttered something below his breath, and once more tried to edge away.

'Now don't you be in such a hurry,' said Mr. Budd and signed to the landlord to refill the empty glass. 'You just have a sociable drink and tell me how things are goin'. What are you doin' in this part of the world? Havin' a holiday?'

'No. I — I came down to see a relation of mine who lives in the neighbourhood,' said Mr. Larkin sullenly.

'A relation, eh? Never thought you had any. Did Harry Milton come down to see this relation of yours, too?'

Mr. Larkin was a little taken aback at this question.

' 'Arry Milton?' he said uneasily. 'I don't know anythin' about 'im.'

'Queer,' said the big man, swirling the beer in his tankard thoughtfully. 'And you and Harry used to be such good friends.'

'That was a long time ago,' said the other quickly. ' 'Arry's been inside.'

'I know he's been inside,' said Mr. Budd. 'And you might call him inside out. Harry Milton was shot last night. Did you know that?'

'No — yes. I — I dunno.' The little thief was incoherent.

'Well, make up your mind,' said Mr. Budd, 'did you know or didn't you?'

'I — I heard somebody had been shot and — ' Mr. Larkin stopped and licked his dry lips.

' — and you guessed it was Harry Milton,' finished the big man. 'So you was down here last night.'

'No, I wasn't!' said Mr. Larkin loudly. 'And you can't prove I was! What's the meanin' of all these questions? You've no right to question me! You know that!'

'Question you?' murmured Mr. Budd, with an air of great innocence. 'Come now, Sid. You can't say I've been questionin' you? You can't call it 'question'' to hold a little light conversation with an old friend.'

'Yes, I know,' snarled Larkin. 'I know your little light conversation. I've had some. The next thing you do is pinch a feller.'

'I wouldn't pinch you,' protested the Superintendent. 'You know me better than that. Besides, what have you got to pinch you for? You didn't shoot Harry Milton,' did you?'

'Is that what you're tryin' to pull on me?' said the other, and there was fear in his small eyes. 'Is that the idea, eh?'

'So far as I'm concerned,' said Mr, Budd, 'there's no idea. I'd just like to know what Harry was doin' round here to get himself shot.'

'I don't know nothin' about it. I've told you I don't!' protested Larkin, looking

96

uneasily about him.

'How have you been doin' since Joe Rennett died?' asked Mr. Budd. 'You used to do pretty well working for him didn't you?'

'Look here, what are you drivin' at?' demanded Larkin, and his fear was pathetic, 'I dunno what you mean. I did one or two jobs for Joe, yes. There's no secret about that. You pulled me in for one of 'em. But I dunno know nothin' about Joe Rennett, nor 'Arry Milton — '

'Nor Bob Smillit,' murmured Mr. Budd softly.

The man before him went a pasty grey.

'Nor Bob Smillit,' he mumbled. 'Who's he, anyway?'

'He's the feller who took over Joe Rennet's cottage after he disappeared,' said the big man. 'And he was killed the day before last. Bashed on the head, in his own sittin' room. You don't know anythin' about that, either. I suppose?'

Mr. Larkin reached out a trembling hand, picked up his glass, and swallowed the contents at a gulp.

'No, I dunno nothin', and I'm not goin'

to stop 'ere and be questioned by you. I'm goin', see?'

'Just a minute!' Once again a big restraining hand was laid on his arm. 'You're too anxious to run away, Sid. I think you and I had better get together and have a little chat. Not here, but in some place that's a bit more private.'

Mr. Larkin's eyes narrowed.

'What's this?' he demanded. 'A cop?'

'No.' The fat detective shook his head. 'But it may be if you aren't reasonable. I believe you can be useful to me Sid, and if you are, well, I'm not pressin' any charges. So what about it?'

The little man fingered his bristling moustache nervously.

'It don't seem that I've got much choice,' he muttered. 'All right. I'll come with yer. Where are we goin'.'

'Not very far,' said Mr. Budd. 'Just you wait a minute while I speak to Sergeant Leek.'

'What?' exclaimed Mr. Larkin. 'Is 'e 'ere too? Blimey! The whole of Scotland Yard seems to be 'ere!'

'The best part of it,' murmured the big

man gently. 'The best part of it, Sid.'

He moved over to where the lean sergeant was still sipping his lime juice.

'Follow me along to the cottage,' he whispered, and Leek nodded. 'Now then,' said Mr. Budd, 'we'll just go and have a cosy chat.'

He slipped his arm affectionately through the thin Mr. Larkin's and piloted him out of the bar, watched by a battery of curious eyes.

'It's a lucky thing I met you,' he continued, as they walked along towards Mr. Mutch's cottage, and the man by his side grunted.

'Is it?' he growled dubiously.

'It is,' said Mr. Budd. 'Otherwise you might have been gettin' yourself into trouble, Sid. Now if you're a wise feller you'll just spill the beans and skip.'

There's nothin' you can hang on me!' declared Sid Larkin.

'Get it out of your head that I'm tryin' to hang anythin' on you,' retorted the Superintendent impatiently. 'I'm not. All I want is the truth.'

They covered the rest of the distance in

silence, and presently reached their destination. The front door was open, but Mr. Mutch was no longer on guard at the porch. Mr. Budd heard him talking to his wife as he entered the little hall, and called through.

'I'm just takin' a friend of mine upstairs,' he said.

The door was opened and Mr. Mutch appeared silhouetted against the light.

'All right, Mr. B.,' he mumbled. 'Be wantin' anythin'?'

'No, thank you,' said the big man, and pushed his nervous companion up the narrow staircase.

When they were seated in the tiny bedroom he took one of his cigars, lit it carefully, and surveyed Larkin through half closed eyes.

'Now, Sid,' he said, 'just let's have it. All of it! Don't go wastin' any more time sayin' you don't know this and you don't know that. Just tell me what you're doin' in Avernly.'

Mr. Larkin rubbed his bristly chin and frowned.

'Look 'ere,' he said, after a pause, 'you

ain't goin' to remember anythin' I says against me, is that a bargain?'

'It all depends,' said Mr. Budd. 'If you've got anythin' to do with these two killin's I can't promise it, and you know I can't. But if you haven't, well, I'm not a hard man.'

The other fetched a sigh of relief.

'Well, that's all right,' he said. 'I don't know nothing' about the killin's. I'll tell you all about it. As you know, I used to work for Joe, 'elped 'im in one or two of 'is busts. It was money for jam, for Joe was always a safe feller to work for. 'E looked after 'imself and 'e looked after the people wot was with 'im. And there was always an alibi for all of us. Mind you, I never knew much about 'im. 'E kept 'isself to 'isself, and when 'e wanted any of us 'e knew where to find us. I was with 'im on that American bank business. And now I've told you somethin' that you can get me a laggin' for.' He stopped, and looked inquiringly at the big man, but Mr. Budd only smiled.

'Go on,' he said. 'We'll talk about that laggin' later.'

'Well, after the bank business,' went on Mr. Larkin, 'Joe disappeared. 'E was supposed to meet us three nights after and pay us our share. You could always rely on Joe keepin' 'is word, and when 'e didn't turn up we thought 'e'd either been pinched or somethin' was wrong somewhere. And then we saw in the papers about 'is bein' killed, and we said goodbye to our money.'

'Who's we?' murmured the Superintendent, and Mr. Larkin shook his head.

'I don't mind talkin' about meself,' he declared, 'but I ain't givin' any other person away. As I said, we didn't know much about Joe, and the only person who did was in bird, 'Arry Milton. We knew the money 'adn't been discovered, but we'd no idea what Joe 'ad done with it. We always guessed 'e 'ad a 'idcout somewhere, but nobody, except 'Arry Milton, knew where it was. We sort of crossed off the American bank business as a bad debt, if you understand what I mean, and we'd almost forgotten about it when 'Arry came out of prison. 'E'd 'eard about Joe's fate and the missin' money

— you know 'ow these things get to the ears of convicts — and the first thing 'e did was to come and see us and say that 'e reckoned 'e knew where the money was. Naturally we was interested. 'E said that if we liked to 'elp 'im lay 'is 'ands on it there'd be a cut for all of us. 'E said Joe 'ad rented a little cottage in the country and it was there that 'e'd most likely 'id the money. 'E said if I'd meet 'im at the Avernly Arms 'e'd show me the place. 'E didn't want none of the others 'cause 'e said that two of us 'ud be quite enough for the job, and a lot of strangers about the place might look suspicious.

'I was to meet 'im there tonight. Well, I come down at the time 'e said and got talking to a feller in a pub near the station where I popped in to 'ave a quick one, the journey 'avin' made me dry. And 'e told me that a feller called Milton 'ad been shot.'

He paused, moistened his lips, and went on:

'It put the wind up me, I can tell you, and my first idea was to 'op on a train and go back 'ome. Then I thought p'raps it might be another Milton. I came along to the Avernly Arms where 'e'd arranged to meet me and ran into you. Now that's gospel, and that's all I knows!'

From under his heavy lids Mr. Budd eyed him keenly, and came to the conclusion that the man was speaking the truth.

'So Milton must have come ahead of you?'

'I suppose 'e must,' said Mr. Larkin. 'Though you can take it from me 'e weren't tryin' no funny business. 'Arry was straight with 'is pals. Maybe 'e thought 'e'd spy out the ground.'

'And you've no idea who shot him?' said Mr. Budd.

The little man shook his head.

'No I ain't!' he declared. 'You could 'ave knocked me down with a feather when I 'eard 'e'd been bumped off. Now you can pinch me if you like, though we've got no witnesses and I shall deny everythin' I've said to you if you bring me up before the beak.'

'I'm not goin' to pinch you, Sid,' said Mr. Budd. 'I'm after bigger game than you.'

He put a series of questions, which Mr. Larkin answered to the best of his ability, but they resulted in bringing him no nearer to the identity of the person who had shot Harry Milton and presumably killed Bob Smillit than he had been before. The shadowy killer was still a mystery, as unsubstantial as the darkness outside the window of his little room.

9

The empty cottage

The difficulty that now presented itself was what to do with Mr. Larkin. It was essential that he should keep that nervous man under observation, and therefore it was impossible to allow him to carry out his frankly expressed wish to return to Town. After a little argument he prevailed upon him to let Sergeant Leek fix a room at the Avernly Arms, and Mr. Larkin accepted this proposal when he discovered that the alternative was a cell in Sellington Police Station.

The man had gone, accompanied by the lean sergeant, when an unexpected visitor arrived in the person of Doctor Carr. His face was pale and troubled when Mr. Budd came down and interviewed him in the little parlour where Mrs. Mutch had shown him.

'You wish to see me — ' began the big

man, and the doctor interrupted him quickly.

'Yes,' he replied. 'I'm worried. Very worried. It's about Miss Brade.'

Mr. Budd's eyes opened to their widest extent.

'Miss Brade?' he repeated.

'Yes,' went on the doctor, speaking rapidly. 'I'm afraid something's happened to her.' He was pacing the room with quick, nervous strides. 'We'd arranged to go for a walk. I was to call for her at half past nine. But when I got to her cottage I could get no reply. The place was in darkness.'

'Maybe she's out,' suggested Mr. Budd, reasonably.

The doctor shook his head impatiently.

'If anything had transpired to make her change her plans she would have let me know,' he answered. 'She always has. Either telephoned or called round to the surgery.' It crossed the big man's mind to wonder whether the girl had cleared out. It was not an improbable thing if she was, as he believed, mixed up in this affair. He kept this thought, however, to himself.

'Why should you think anythin' has happened?' he inquired, and Carr frowned and bit his lips.

'I don't know,' he declared. 'But — well, ever since I've known her I've thought there was some — some mystery about her.'

The big man thought so, too, although he realized that the young doctor's answer was more or less in the nature of a subterfuge. What he was really worried about was the fact that he had recognised the girl's handkerchief as the one the stout Superintendent had found in Smillit's garden after the murder, and although he had said nothing, was wondering whether she was connected with the crime. It was obvious that Doctor Carr had a deeper interest in the girl than mere friendship.

'What do you want me to do?' he asked slowly.

'I don't know — perhaps I was a fool to come here, but, well, I've got a feeling something's wrong. I thought perhaps you might come up to Holly House and see what you think.' He spoke jerkily and nervously. 'I — I didn't want to go to Buckle. For one thing you're nearer . . . '

'I'll come along,' said Mr. Budd, making up his mind, for he was almost as interested in the movements of the girl as the man before him.

'It's up by the Green,' said Carr. 'It won't take us more than twenty minutes.'

The big man fetched his hat, gave a brief word of explanation to Mr. Mutch, and started out with his worried companion.

Holly House was a small, thatched cottage, standing back on the north side of the Green. It had a trim little garden in front, surrounded by a high hedge of the prickly bush from which it derived its name. The place was in complete darkness, and when they stood under the little porch they could hear no sound. Carr raised his hand and knocked. There was no answer. After a moment or two he knocked again, with the same result.

'She's evidently not at home,' murmured Mr. Budd. 'Can we get round to the back?'

His companion nodded and led the

way round the side of the building. The back was also in darkness, but when he tried the handle of a door, which opened into the small garden he found that it was unlocked.

'If we go in we shall be trespassing,' he remarked, 'but since you're a friend of the young lady's and willin' to take the responsibility I don't mind.'

'Yes, yes! Never mind about trespassing,' said the doctor impatiently. 'What I'm anxious to do is to find out if anything's happened to Olivia.'

He struck a match as they crossed the threshold and by its feeble glimmer they made their way through a neat kitchen to a passage that led to the rest of the building. At the foot of the crooked staircase Mr. Budd sniffed.

'Can you smell anything?' he asked, and the doctor's voice was hoarse as he replied.

'Yes. Chloroform!'

'I thought that, too,' murmured the big man. 'Is there a lamp anywhere?'

'On the table in the hall,' answered Carr, and dropping the match which was burning his fingers struck another. He found the lamp and lit it, and as he turned up the wick and the little hall became filled with light they saw that a rug on the floor was crumpled up and a chair overturned.

'See that?' whispered Carr huskily. 'Something *has* happened to her. I was right!'

'I think you were,' said Mr. Budd, and his face was grave.

He stooped in a corner and picked up a white object, which was damp to his touch. It was a wad of lint and still smelt strongly.

'Somebody knocked,' he murmured. 'Miss Brade went to the door, and they overpowered her and chloroformed her.'

'Who could it be?' Carr's face was yellow in the lamplight. 'Who could it be? What have they done with her?'

The big man made no reply, he was peering about.

'What did you know of Miss Brade?' he inquired, looking up suddenly.

'Nothing, except that I was engaged to be married to her,' answered the doctor.

111

'I see. You didn't know her before she came here?'

Carr shook his head.

'You remember that handkerchief I found in the garden of Smillit's cottage,' went on Mr. Budd. 'That was Miss Brade's, wasn't it?'

The doctor hesitated.

'Don't go hidin' things up, sir,' said the Superintendent. 'You'd much better be frank, especially now.'

'Well, yes, it was,' said Carr, reluctantly.

'I thought so. Did Miss Brade know about that?'

The doctor shook his head again.

'No,' he answered. 'It's been on the tip of my tongue to ask her over and over again, but I thought — well, maybe, I'd been mistaken. After all, she couldn't be mixed up in that business.'

'Well, she was certainly in that garden,' said Mr. Budd, with conviction. 'And she must have had some reason for bein' there. However, we won't discuss that now. What we've got to do is to find out where she's gone.'

He opened the front door and stared

down at the step, but it was of red brick and bore no impression. Neither, he saw, would the little paved path which led down to the gate. The only possibility was the roadway. He walked down to the gate and out on to the pavement, and at the kerb he found a little spot of black oil, and pursed his lips.

'She was taken in a car,' he muttered to the agitated doctor who hovered at his elbow, 'and it didn't wait very long or there'd have been more oil. Now, where was she taken to?'

'Good Lord, man!' burst out Carr 'What can we do? Supposing she's in the hands of this fellow who killed those two men?'

'If she is I don't suppose she's hurt much,' said the fat detective consolingly. 'If the intention had been to kill her she'd have been killed here.'

He struck a match and examined the roadway, and as he straightened up there was a curious expression on his big face. One of his greatest assets was an abnormal memory for small details Anything he had once seen he never forgot, and he had seen something now which recalled an incident that left him wondering and a little breathless.

'Go and put the lamp out and shut up the cottage,' he said, and there was a new tone to his voice that made Carr look at him sharply. 'We don't want to advertise our presence here to anyone who may pass by.'

'But what about Olivia — ' began the young doctor, and Mr. Budd interrupted him.

'You leave that to me,' he said. 'I think I can guarantee to find her before morning.'

'You can?' exclaimed Carr eagerly. 'Why? What did you see in the gutter — '

'Now don't go worrying me by askin' questions,' said the big Superintendent wearily. 'Just you go and shut up the cottage and then go quietly home and wait until you hear from me.'

'But,' exclaimed Carr, 'you can't expect me — '

'Look here, sir,' said Mr. Budd quickly. 'I've got a lot of thinkin' and a lot of work to do, and you're only hinderin' me. If you leave me alone and do as I tell you I'll find this girl of yours, and I'll find her before she comes to any harm.'

'All right,' said Carr shortly. 'I'll do as you wish.'

'I'll get in touch with you directly I've got any news,' promised Mr. Budd, and to the doctor's surprise turned and hurried away across the Green.

He had been right when he said he had a lot of thinking to do, and his brain worked rapidly as he walked. It was incredible, but there was no doubt, and as he reviewed the case in the light of the fresh knowledge, which had come to him it grew clearer and clearer. With the exception of a few minor details he guessed the whole solution.

The perspiration was pouring down his fat face when he reached Mr. Mutch's cottage and found Leek.

'Get on to Sergeant Buckle,' he ordered, 'and tell him I want as many men as he can muster to meet me here as soon as possible.'

The lean man's jaw dropped and he stared in open-eyed amazement.

'What for?' he demanded.

'We're goin' to pull in the man who shot Harry Milton and killed Bob Smillit tonight!' snapped Mr. Budd, and Leek was so astonished that he forgot to argue for once, and went running towards the Avernly Arms to carry out his instructions.

The stout Superintendent sat down on the porch seat to recover his breath. He was taking a risk, a big risk. The tiny fact on which he had based his convictions would scarcely be enough to put before a jury. It was sufficient to satisfy him, but unless he could discover substantiating evidence he was going to find himself in trouble. Only for an instant did he hesitate, however, and then his jaw set. The evidence would be forthcoming. It must be forthcoming! At least the charge of abduction could be proved.

He went in, found Mr. Mutch, and to that surprised man put a question.

'Near the bottom of the 'igh Street, Mr. B. It's quite a large place, standin' in its own grounds.'

'I guessed it would be,' grunted the big

man. 'Yes, it 'ud have to be standing in its own grounds.'

He walked away, leaving the old man under the impression that he had been drinking. It was half an hour later when a police car drew up outside the cottage, and Sergeant Buckle, accompanied by four stalwart constables, came up the little path. Mr. Budd met them at the porch, and drawing the sergeant to one side began to speak rapidly.

Buckle's red face grew more and more amazed as he proceeded.

'I suppose you're sure of this, Superintendent?' he inquired, when the big man had finished. 'It's going to be mighty awkward for us if you're wrong.'

'I'm not wrong!' declared Mr. Budd. 'You'll find all the evidence you'll need at the house.'

The sergeant pursed his lips.

'Well, sir,' he said, 'it's your responsibility. I've got instructions from Superintendent McNeill to give you all the assistance you want.'

'Good!' snapped Mr. Budd. 'Then let's start. Have you got room in that machine

117

of yours or shall I fetch me own?'

'I think we can all squeeze in, sir,' said the sergeant.

He shepherded his men back to the car and they managed, with difficulty, to make room for Leek and the fat detective. The car moved off, and wedged uncomfortably between two bucolic policemen, Mr. Budd wondered whether the next two hours would see him triumphant or awaiting the severe reprimand which would be his if he was wrong.

10

The man responsible

The night was mild and moonless, and in a narrow lane that turned off the lower end of the High Street the police driver stopped the car at Mr. Budd's instructions.

'We'll go on foot from here,' said the big Superintendent. 'The place isn't very far, is it?'

'No, sir,' answered Sergeant Buckle. 'The drive entrance is about a 'undred yards further on, on the right 'and side.'

The fat detective nodded.

'Get your men and follow me,' he said. 'I'll take Sergeant Leek with me. You post your men so that they can command every exit from the house. They're to stop anybody who attempts to leave, though unless I'm very much mistaken there are only two people there, and one isn't in a condition to leave without assistance.'

'If you've made a mistake, sir,' said the

119

worried Buckle, 'there's goin' to be a 'ell of a row over this!'

'I know!' said Mr. Budd shortly. 'But it won't affect you. If there's any kicks comin' I shall get 'em!'

They had reached the drive gates, and turning into the dark avenue made their way towards the dim bulk of the house that was faintly visible against the deep blue of the Summer sky.

'There's a grass edgin',' whispered the stout Superintendent. 'Keep on that and it'll deaden our footsteps.'

They came presently to where the drive curved in a semi-circle before the front entrance, and here he stopped, to issue final instructions to Buckle. Whatever the sergeant may have been privately thinking, he allowed none of his misgivings to stand in the way of his complete obedience. He and the men with him melted into the shadows of the grounds, and in the shelter of a bush Mr. Budd waited with the lugubrious figure of Leek, quivering with excitement, at his side.

'Gosh, I 'ope you ain't made a bloomer!' whispered the sergeant. 'They'll 'ave your coat off your back for this if you 'ave!'

'Try bein' an optimist for a change!' snarled Mr. Budd, whose nerves were on edge. 'Now, we'll wait a quarter of an hour and then we'll knock.'

Never had such a short period of time passed so slowly. It seemed an eternity before the hands of his watch showed him that fifteen minutes had elapsed since Buckle and his men had gone to take up their positions.

'Now!' he said. 'Come on, and let's hope for the best!'

With Leek at his heels he crossed cautiously over the intervening crescent of gravel leading up to the front door. For a moment he hesitated, his hand on the knocker, and then gave a sharp tattoo and waited.

There was no reply. No light showed through the leaded panes at the side of the massive portal and no footstep from within heralded the approach of anyone to answer his summons.

He was a little relieved. Had there been any servants they would have already come to see who knocked, and the absence of servants tended to confirm his theory.

He knocked again more loudly, a peremptory rat-tat-tat, and this time with more success. There came a sound from within the silent house and a light sprang up in the hall. There was the click of a latch and the door was pulled open.

'Who is that?' inquired a throaty voice.

'Good evenin', Mr. Thrussel,' said Mr. Budd. 'Can I have a word with you, sir?'

The bank manager peered uncertainly at the bulky figure of the fat detective.

'Good gracious me,' he said. 'It's Superintendent Budd.'

'That's right,' answered the big man. 'I'd just like to have a little chat, if you're not busy.'

To all intents and purposes he was alone. Leek, acting on instructions, had pressed himself up against the side of the porch and in the shadows was invisible to the man in the hall.

'I was — er — just going to bed,' said Mr. Thrussel pompously. 'Really, Super-intendent, it's a little late — '

'I won't keep you very long,' broke in

Mr. Budd, 'but it's rather important.'

Mr. Thrussel frowned.

'Very well,' he said at last, after some hesitation. 'But I really must ask you to curtail your visit. I am exceedingly tired and it was my intention to retire early.'

'Very wise,' murmured Mr. Budd, as he stepped across the threshold. 'Nothin' like retirin' early.'

The stout figure of the man before him was fully dressed, and led the way across the hall to a room on the right.

'Come into my study,' he said, and switched on the light.

Mr. Budd made to follow him into the comfortably furnished room, and then, in some confusion, remembered his hat.

'Excuse me,' he muttered, and removing the hard derby returned and set it down on the hallstand. 'Not used to callin' at gentlemen's houses,' he apologized, coming back to the study. 'Nice place you've got here, Mr. Thrussel.'

'Yes, yes, quite — er — adequate,' said the bank manager. He was rather ill at ease and nervous. 'Now then, Superintendent, what can I do for you?'

'It's rather a delicate matter,' murmured the big man, closing the door, 'and I wouldn't like anyone to overhear us.'

'That's quite all right, you needn't worry at all,' broke in Mr. Thrussel. 'My servants have gone to a concert at Sellington. I had some complimentary tickets, which I gave them. What is this matter on which you wish to see me so urgently?'

'Well, sir,' said Mr. Budd, 'it's like this. I'm given to understand that you were acquainted with this feller who owned Smillit's cottage before it became empty.'

'I?' Mr. Thrussel's eyebrows rose and his round face was the picture of astonishment. 'My dear sir. Who told you that? I never met the man in my life!'

Mr. Budd looked slightly disappointed.

'Somebody seems to have been givin' me wrong information,' he muttered. 'I was told you knew him quite well. And since naturally we're tryin' to find out all we can concernin' the place I was hopin' you'd be able to help me.'

'I'm afraid you've come to the wrong man,' replied the bank manager. 'I know of him, of course, but that's all. So far as I'm concerned, Superintendent, I'm afraid I can't help you at all.'

'That's very disappointin'. Very disappointin' indeed.' The fat detective's face fell and he shook his head. 'Oh, well, I'm sorry to have troubled you, sir.' He wandered disconsolately round the room.

'No trouble, no trouble at all,' said Mr. Thrussel, watching him impatiently. 'I only wish I could have been of service.'

'Nice place you've got here,' murmured Mr. Budd conversationally. 'Must cost a lot to keep up a house like this.'

'A fair amount,' said the other. 'Luckily I'm not entirely dependent upon my salary. I have a private income.'

'I often wish I had,' said the big man, shaking his head sadly. 'It must be a nice feelin', sir, to know that you haven't got to worry about money.'

He rambled on, passing from one subject to another, until Mr. Thrussel could barely conceal his impatience. At last he broke in on a rather long-winded account of Mr. Budd's ambitions when he retired.

'Yes, yes. I've no doubt that would be very nice,' he said. 'I'm sorry to hurry you, Superintendent, but as I mentioned when you first came, I'm really very tired, and if you'll excuse me — '

'Dear me, I'm very sorry, sir,' said the fat detective. 'I've been keepin' you up. Still, it's not often I get the chance of havin' a little chat to a gentleman like yourself. I'll be gettin' along then. Surely,' — he pointed to a picture on the wall — 'that's a genuine Constable, isn't it?'

'No, no,' said Mr. Thrussel. 'It's a painting by a modern artist.'

'Never was much good at art,' said the big man. 'I suppose it's a gift recognisin' these pictures. I had a brother once,' — this was totally untrue for Mr. Budd had been an only child — 'who used to dabble in that sort of thing, and he gave me one or two tips.'

'Very interesting,' said the bank manager, who was fast losing his patience. 'Good night, Superintendent.'

'Good night, sir,' said Mr. Budd, opening the door and passing out into the hall. 'I'm sorry I've troubled you but,'

— he turned swiftly — 'I'll have to trouble you more. Will you put on your hat and coat, please, and be ready to accompany me to the police station at Sellington!'

Mr. Thrussel started, and his face went grey.

'What — what d'you mean?' he stammered. 'This is an outrage, Superintendent! I shall do nothing of the sort!'

'I think you will,' said Mr. Budd, and his lazy voice had changed to one of authority. 'You'll do exactly as you're told, Mr. Thrussel. You're under arrest and — keep your hand away from your pocket unless you want a bullet through your wrist!' An automatic had appeared in his fat hand, and the bank manager hastily raised the arm that he had been dropping towards his right-hand jacket pocket.

'Really, this is preposterous!' he protested. 'On what charge are you arresting me?'

'On a charge of abduction!' snapped the big man, and without turning his head called: 'You've found her, Leek?'

127

The melancholy sergeant appeared in the doorway.

'Yes, she's upstairs,' he answered. 'In a small room on the second floor. Unconscious and bound hand and foot,'

Thrussel's face was the colour of dirty putty.

'How — how did you get in?' he mumbled.

'I let him in,' said Mr. Budd calmly, 'when I went to hang up my hat in the hall. I shouldn't advise you to give any trouble. Abduction is only one charge. There may be others. Go and take that pistol off him,' he continued. 'It's in the pocket of his jacket. And if the bullet that killed Harry Milton don't fit I'll hand in me resignation!'

11

Mr. Budd writes his report

Mr. Budd sat in his cheerless office at Scotland Yard on the afternoon of the following day, an unlighted cigar in the corner of his mouth, and laboriously wrote his report . . .

' . . . It was not until the abduction of Miss Olivia Brade that I got the first clue to the person behind the murders of Robert Smillit and Harold Milton. When I examined the roadway outside her cottage on the night of her disappearance I saw the marks of a tyre in a patch of mud that had not quite dried. There was a zig-zag tear in the tread and I remembered having seen a similar mark in Thorn Lane, on the morning of Smillit's murder, made by Mr. Thrussel's car.

'In the ordinary course of events I

should have waited to acquire more evidence before taking the steps which I did, but I was afraid that any delay might place Miss Brade in serious danger, and I decided to act at once. After surrounding the house I called on Thrussel and without his knowing succeeded in admitting Sergeant Leek. I kept Thrussel engaged in conversation while Sergeant Leek searched the house, and I knew I had made no mistake when I learned that the servants had all been sent away that evening.

'Sergeant Leek discovered, as I expected, Miss Brade, unconscious and securely bound in an upstairs bedroom, and I immediately arrested Thrussel on a charge of abduction.

'A search of the house by Sergeant Buckle and myself brought to light a stout, iron-bound box which, on being opened, was found to contain five hundred thousand dollars in one thousand dollar bills, and a quantity of English currency amounting to a further four thousand five hundred pounds.

'Thrussel refused to make any statement

until he was confronted with the evidence of the bullet extracted from Milton's skull. This, as I expected, exactly fitted the revolver that was taken from him at the time of his arrest, and there is no doubt that it was with that weapon that he shot Milton in Thorn Lane. When he found that the evidence against him was overwhelming he made the statement, which I append to this report.

'Miss Brade recovered consciousness shortly after Sergeant Leek found her, and later also made a statement, a copy of which is appended herewith, and explains fully her position in the case.

'The evidence necessary for the conviction of Thrussel is in the hands of Superintendent McNeill and I understand the case will come up for hearing at the next session of the Oxfordshire Assizes.

'ROBERT BUDD,
'Superintendent, C.I.D.'

The stout man read through what he had written, attached two other documents to it with a clip, and rang for a messenger.

When he had dispatched it to the Assistant Commissioner's room he lighted his cigar and leaned back in his chair with a sigh of relief.

Colonel Blair received the report, and after deciphering Mr. Budd's sprawling calligraphy with difficulty turned his attention to the two appended statements. The first one began:

'I make this statement of my own free will and without any coercion on the part of the police.

'My name is Olivia Millicent Brade and I am a citizen of the United States of America, employed by the Wakefield Detective Agency. My firm was approached by the Bankers' Association of New York to inquire into the matter of the missing five hundred thousand dollars stolen from the London Branch of the American Exchange Bank by Joseph Rennett. The Head Office of the bank were under the impression that the reason the money had not been recovered was due to connivance on the part of the English police,'
— the Assistant Commissioner uttered

an indignant snort — 'and I was instructed, when I was sent over to England, not to disclose my identity to the English Detective Bureau.

'There is no need for me to go into details concerning my inquiries, but I was able to discover that Rennett had been constantly seen in the neighbourhood of Avernly, and that it was believed he had a hideout there. I was in a better position to acquire this information than the police themselves, for being female no one suspected that I was a detective, and therefore I was able to conduct my inquiries among Rennett's associates without arousing their suspicion.

'I came to Avernly and took up my residence at Holly House. It was some time before I was able to discover that Pine Cottage was the hideout used by Joseph Rennett during his operations. I did not discover this until after the cottage had been rented by Robert Smillit. My principal task was to find the money. That was all my employers were interested in, and having found the cottage I believed that some clue to the whereabouts of the five hundred thousand dollars was concealed in it. On two occasions I managed to effect an entry and searched the place without disturbing Smillit, but I failed to find what I was looking for. On the third occasion I came to the cottage and found that someone had forestalled me. The place had been broken into and Smillit lay dead in the sitting room. I was horrified at the discovery and for the moment almost decided to notify the police. Then I thought possibly the murder of Smillit had been committed by an associate of Rennet's who, like myself, was looking for the five hundred thousand dollars.

'I made up my mind to be silent and let the crime be discovered by someone else.

'Although I did not at first connect him with the business on which I had come to England, ever since I had taken up my residence in Avernly I had been suspicious of Mr. Thrussel. His house and general standard of living was far beyond the resources of a bank manager's salary. I was under the impression that in some way he was robbing his employers, but it was not until the night that Smillit was killed that I began to suspect him of being connected with that. After I had left Pine Cottage I met him hurrying home. He recognised me and made some excuse about being unable to sleep and having come out for a walk. But he was agitated, and I wondered. I could not see how he could be mixed up with the affair and I thought perhaps I was allowing my imagination to run away with me. I was soon to discover this was not so.

'During my residence in Avernly I had become friendly with Doctor Carr. At first I did this because I thought he might be useful, but later I came to value his friendship. We had arranged that he should call for me after surgery and that we should go for a walk, which we had often done before. I was waiting for him when a knock came at the door, and thinking it was Doctor Carr I went out into the hall to admit him. As soon as the door was opened somebody sprang at me, and before I could defend myself a pad of chloroform was forced over my mouth and nostrils. I struggled violently, but the drug took effect, and that's all I remember until I found myself lying on a narrow bed in a small bedroom with Doctor Carr and Sergeant Leek looking down at me.'

The statement was signed with a bold 'Olivia Brade' and witnessed by 'George Buckle, Sergeant, Oxfordshire Constabulary,' and 'William Leek, Sergeant, C.I.D.'

The assistant Commissioner rubbed his chin gently, laid the statement aside and picked up the second.

'My name is John Hamilton Thrussel and I make this statement at my own request without pressure from the police.

'My age is fifty-two, I am a British subject and unmarried. I began my business career as a clerk in the Lombard Street Branch of the Southern Counties Bank. I was always of an extravagant nature and more than once found myself in difficulties with moneylenders. On more than one occasion I was nearly discovered appropriating the funds of the bank, but I managed to stave off discovery by speculation, which, luckily for me, enabled me to cover up my misdemeanours. I was promoted to cashier and eventually to the management of the Avernly branch. This responsible position placed me in the way of temptation. I was fond of good living and display and I used funds that did not belong to me in order to gratify it. I plunged heavily on the Stock Exchange and one way and another got myself thoroughly in the mire. I reckoned that I could evade detection for another twelve months, but unless a miracle happened at the end of that time I should be arrested.

'I was planning a desperate expedient to extricate me from my financial difficulties by a further gamble in shares when, driving back from a party in London I ran into a man on a motor cycle. The collision did little damage to my own car, but he was travelling at a high speed and his machine crashed into a tree at the side of the road, killing him instantly.

'His injuries were terrible, and even now I shudder at the memory. I had no intention, however, of getting mixed up with an accident that would only add to my troubles. What made me search the man I don't know. I think it may have been a hope that perhaps he was carrying something of value that might ease my present situation, for I was desperately hard-up.

'I found a few pounds and a red notebook, bearing the name Joseph Rennett on the inside flap. I knew then who it was I had killed, the bank robber whom the police suspected of so many daring raids. The book contained a jumble of letters and figures and I could see they formed some kind of cipher. I put the thing in my pocket and drove away from the scene as quickly as I could.

'It was not until two days after that I learned Rennett was suspected of having got away with five hundred thousand dollars from the American Exchange Bank, and that no trace of this sum had been discovered. It occurred to me that the whereabouts of the missing money might be contained in the notebook I had taken from the dead man. If this was so, and I could find out where it was hidden, it would mean not only that I should be able to save myself from ruin and disgrace, but that I should have enough left to start life again abroad; enough to live for the rest of my days in luxury.

'But I could make nothing of the cipher. For nearly twelve months I worked every night on that jumble of figures and letters, trying desperately to find a solution. A cipher expert would probably have done so in less time than I took, but I had to work it out on my own since for obvious reasons it was impossible to engage the services of such a man.

'Eventually I succeeded. Quite a lot of it consisted of notes and plans for robberies which didn't interest me at all, but there was one portion which made me catch my breath, for I had found what I was seeking,

'Rennett had cachéd his money in one of the old gravel pits at the end of Thorn Lane, and the exact whereabouts was revealed by a calendar in Pine Cottage.

'I had heard of the two burglaries which had taken place there, and I wondered whether some associate of Rennet's hadn't forestalled me. I spent two whole evenings searching the quarry, but without discovering any trace of the missing money or the place where Rennett had hidden it, and I concluded that without the clue mentioned — the calendar — I might go on searching for months.

'The following night I decided to break into the cottage and look for this calendar. I was searching for it when Smillit disturbed me. His astonishment when he recognised me would have been funny if it hadn't been so serious. I realised that I was done for if he mentioned he'd caught me searching his place, and picking up a hammer that he'd apparently been using I hit him several times. He died without a sound. I was horrified at what I'd done but it was the only way.

'I set to work to find what I'd come for. I found it eventually, tucked away behind some plates on the dresser. It was an old calendar, dusty and dirty, and bore a picture of the quarry. An ex-service man came to Avernly two years before and sold quite a lot of these calendars, bearing photographs of various points of interest. There was a tiny pencil mark when I examined the picture closely, over a clump of bushes, and I knew I'd got the clue I wanted.

'On an impulse I made the place look as though it had been thoroughly searched, my intention being to make the police think more than one person had been concerned. And then I left, taking the hammer with me, for it bore my fingerprints. Just before Smillit had discovered me I had taken off one of my gloves to screw up the bulb of the torch I was carrying.

'I'd have collected the money that

night only I felt too nervy.

'On my way home I overtook Miss Brade, who recognised me. That worried me a lot after. The following night I went to the quarry.

'The marked bushes were thick and dense, and in the middle of them I found a ring, half buried in the earth. I tugged at this and a square trap or lid came up, revealing a cavity about two feet square, in which was an iron bound box. I knew I had found the money, though when I came to lift it, it wasn't very heavy. I'd left my car in a field where I knew it would be safe from discovery, and I was coming along Thorn Lane when a man flew out of the gate of Pine Cottage and accosted me. I didn't know who he was. I thought for a moment he might be a detective. 'What have you got there?' he demanded. Before he could say anything else I pulled a pistol from my pocket, clapped it to his head, and fired. He collapsed on the strip of grass at the side of the lane, and in terror lest the shot had been heard, I picked up the box and hurried to the car.

'My only worry now was Olivia Brade. I'd heard that a woman's handkerchief had been found at Pine Cottage, and although I couldn't conceive what she'd been doing there I wondered if perhaps she hadn't seen me strike down Smillit. I decided that my safest course was to get rid of her. The plan I carried out was suggested to me by hearing her make an appointment with Doctor Carr in the post office. I sent the servants away with tickets for a concert, called round ten minutes before Doctor Carr was due, drugged her, carried her to my car, and drove her home. I'd have killed her at Holly House only I was afraid Carr might turn up before I could complete the job.

'It may sound strange but I couldn't bring myself to use violence against the girl. My intention was to give her an overdose of chloroform and hide her body that night in the quarry. Few people go there so it would probably have been months before she was discovered.'

The statement ended here, and the Assistant Commissioner frowned at the bold signature. After a thoughtful pause he pressed a button and issued an order to the messenger who came in answer to the summons. After a little delay there was a tap on the door and Mr. Budd came ponderously into the room.

'Sit down, Superintendent,' said Colonel Blair. 'I must congratulate you on a very nice piece of work. The American Exchange Bank have made a great deal of trouble over that money, and I'm very glad it's cleared up.' He fingered the documents before him. 'What's going to happen to this girl, Miss Brade? I suppose she'll go back to America.'

Mr. Budd shook his head and smiled slowly

'I doubt it,' he said. 'I think she's goin' to become a British citizen.'

The Assistant Commissioner looked surprised.

'What makes you think that?' he inquired.

'It's usual for a wife to take on the nationality of her husband,' said the big

Superintendent, 'and if she isn't contemplatin' marryin' Doctor Carr well — ' He
shrugged his massive shoulders.

'I see,' said the Assistant Commissioner. 'Like that, is it?'

'Just like that, sir,' said Mr. Budd.

THE DEVIL'S FOOTPRINT

1

The face in the night

'Well, here we are at last,' remarked Anthony Ware, as he alighted from the train at Scarsgill.

'Yes, sir,' said the short, stocky man who accompanied him, without enthusiasm, glancing dubiously round the desolate station and at the rugged country half seen in the fading light.

The tall, bronzed man by his side looked at him with a whimsical smile.

'I don't seem to detect a whole-hearted enthusiasm for Westmorland, George,' he said.

His servant grimaced and scratched his ear.

'Ain't much life about, is there, sir?' he replied. 'Blimey! It's more sociable in the middle of the African jungle!'

'You've no appreciation of beauty,' said Tony, sniffing the air. 'It may be sombre but it's grand!'

George Binger, Cockney bred and born, made a disparaging sound.

'How about the kit, sir?' he inquired, jerking his head towards the pile of baggage on the platform.

'Kessick should be here to meet us,' answered Tony, looking about. 'Yes, here he comes.'

An elderly man was hobbling towards them, peering through the dusk near-sightedly.

'Is either o' you Mr. Ware?' he inquired wheezily, as he came near to them.

'Surely you haven't forgotten me, Kessick?' greeted Tony Ware with a smile.

The old man's weather-beaten face brightened.

'Mr. Ware it is!' he exclaimed. 'I'm right glad to see ye again, Mr. Tony.'

Ware wrung the gnarled fingers and turned to introduce Binger.

'You've often heard me speak of Kessick,' he said. 'We used to have some rare fun together when I was a boy.'

'Ay, that we did, Master Tony!' chuckled the old man.

'And now we'll have some more,' said

Ware. 'What about the luggage, Kessick?'

'I've brought the old trap, sir,' said Kessick. 'I reckon I can manage.'

'Good! Then Binger and I will walk,' replied Tony. 'I feel like a stretch after being cramped up in the train.'

They left Kessick to deal with the baggage, assisted by the solitary railway official, who combined station-master, porter and ticket collector, and set off on their journey.

The darkness was deepening when they left the village and descended towards Crag Fell. Away in the distance the lights twinkled from Appleby and all around lay the rugged melancholy grey of the moor.

Anthony Ware, who had not seen this place since childhood, was unusually silent, and Binger, who thought he had never seen a more depressing spot before, did not attempt to break in on his master's thoughts.

Presently there was a rattle of hoofs behind them, and turning they saw a decrepit trap driven by Kessick.

The old man hailed them, slowing the pony to a walk.

'You'd better keep by the side of the trap now, sir,' he said. 'We turns up round the corner and t'would be hard for ye to find the way in the dark.'

The side road that he had mentioned was little better than a cart track and wound up between towering crags, which rose black and menacing in the twilight. In a little while they came to more open ground where the track almost lost itself in the heather. But they continued on until the outlines of a wall, behind which towered the leafless branches of trees, came into view. A pair of rusted iron gates stood open and they passed into the gloom of a drive, emerging after a few minutes at the side of the house itself.

Kessick pulled the pony to a halt and clambered stiffly down.

'You give a hand with our gear, George,' said Tony. 'What sort of a staff do we boast here, Kessick?'

'There's only me and my son, Albert, Master Tony,' replied the old man. 'The man was left a house in the will and he's living over Grey Rock way.'

'The man? What man?' Tony's face was

puzzled for a moment then it cleared. 'Oh, of course, you mean my uncle's valet.'

'Yes sir, him what the master brought home from forin parts. He was the only one besides me and Albert.'

Tony nodded, and, leaving them to unload the trap, strolled round to the front of the house.

He wondered what sort of a life his uncle had lived, isolated in the heart of Westmorland. Curiously enough he had never seen the kinsman to whose estate he had succeeded. Like himself, his Uncle Geoffrey seemed to have spent most of his time abroad, and his final homecoming had been in the nature of a tragedy.

Apparently he had only been in occupation a few months when he had met a terrible death in the dreary valley called Crag Fell.

A man was standing in the porch when Tony reached it.

'Good evening, sir,' he said politely, and Ware gave him a shrewd, appraising glance.

He concluded that this was Kessick's son, and there was something about him he didn't like; a shiftiness to his small, closely set, slit-like eyes. Altogether an unpleasant personality, thought Tony as he acknowledged the greeting a little coldly and passed into the hall.

'You'd like a wash, sir, after your journey?' suggested Albert, and led the way up the big staircase.

A fire was burning in the bedroom to which he ushered Tony, the dancing flames throwing weird shadows on the great oak beams of the ceiling. The man had brought an oil lamp with him, and as he set it on the table Ware glanced about the room.

The general effect was melancholy. Grey and sombre; the oak panellings; the dark, thick curtains and carpet; the ancient furniture; all combined to produce an atmosphere that was depressing.

'Is this where my uncle used to sleep?' he asked.

'Yes, sir,' replied Albert. 'It's the best bedroom.'

'Pretty dismal,' commented the new master. 'Not haunted I suppose by any chance?'

He put the question with a smile, but the sudden change of expression on the other's face surprised him. Albert looked apprehensively about him, and drawing closer he said in a low voice, scarcely above a whisper:

'Who told you about — about the ghost, sir?'

'Ghost?' Tony raised his eyebrows incredulously. 'I've heard nothing about a ghost.'

The man shifted uneasily.

'I thought perhaps you'd heard, sir — about the — the face,' he said,

'I've heard nothing,' said Ware. 'Tell me more about this.'

Albert puckered his low forehead.

'P'raps I didn't ought to 'ave said anything,' he muttered. 'But they say as 'ow people who've slept here 'as seen a face, just a face and nothin' else floating about in the dark.'

Tony stared at him, conscious of an unpleasant thrill in the region of his spine, and then reason reasserted itself and he laughed.

'Well,' he laughed presently, drawing an

automatic from his pocket and balancing it on his palm, 'if that face or any other face comes to disturb my sleep it's in for a rough time! I don't like ghosts or anybody else walking about my bedroom in the middle of the night.'

He laid the weapon down on the table by the side of the bed.

'Where's the bathroom?' he continued. 'That interests me more than faces floating about in the dark.'

'I'll show you, sir,' said Albert with obvious relief, and led the way along a dark passage to a door at the end. 'You'll find everything you want there, sir,' he said. 'Is there anything else?'

Anthony shook his head.

'Then I'll go and prepare the dinner,' said the man, and took his departure.

There was plenty of hot water, and when he had washed he went back to the bedroom to find the unromantic figure of Binger unpacking, which did much to dispel the unpleasant impression that the house, and Albert, had created.

By the time he descended, ravenously hungry, to the dining room the matter had more or less slipped from his mind. The cooking was better than he had expected, and when he had finished his meal he filled and lit his pipe with a feeling of content. The prospects of settling down after his adventurous life appealed to him, and although to some the desolate surroundings might have proved a detraction they had no such effect on him. He loved the stern, grey scenery; the grandeur and strength of the great masses of slate rock; the majesty of nature in the raw.

His meditations were interrupted by the arrival of Binger, who came to tell him that he had finished unpacking.

'Thanks,' said Tony. 'How's your room? All fixed up?'

'Yes, sir,' answered the servant. 'I've got the little room at the end of your corridor. There's a bell by your bed that communicates, if you want anything.'

'Splendid!' smiled Anthony, and rising from his chair, he yawned and stretched himself. 'I think I shall turn in early,' he remarked. 'It's too dark, and I'm too tired, to look round the place tonight.'

He knocked the ashes out of his pipe, and, after leaving instructions to be called early, went upstairs.

He grunted as he entered the gloomy bedroom and locked the door, mentally deciding that something must be done to cheer up the interior of the place a bit.

Outside the rising wind howled dismally across the wild expanse, sighing and moaning round the house its boisterousness emphasised by the quietness within.

Dog-tired, he was asleep almost as soon as he got into bed. He had no idea how long he had been asleep when he woke sharply, conscious of a cold draught blowing round him.

He sat up, peering into the pitch blackness with sleep-laden eyes. What had wakened him? He had heard no sound, and then, somewhere over in the corner he glimpsed a faint, luminous radiance.

Even as he stared it grew in volume and there formed in the centre of the nebulous glow a face, a leering mask, emaciated, death-grey . . .

It approached slowly, and as it floated

through the darkness he saw that the corners of the lips were stained — red and horrible, as though blood were oozing . . .

An uncontrollable fear gripped him, and while he gazed, petrified, his throat dry, the cold wind swept round his thinly clad shoulders. Suddenly he thought of the pistol on the table at his side and his courage rushed back. A wave of anger took possession of him as he reached for the weapon, and levelling it at the thing at the foot of the bed pressed the trigger.

The deafening reports were followed by a soft, evil, chuckle, and the face vanished.

Blind, unreasoning fear took hold of Anthony Ware, and seizing the bell-rope that hung behind him he tugged with such violence that it came away in his hand. The stillness of the house was rent by the wild clanging of a bell.

Hurried footsteps came along the corridor and somebody hammered anxiously at the door.

'What's up, Guv'nor? What's the matter?' cried the voice of Binger, and for a moment Tony was too shaken to reply or move. Then, as the servant's voice came again, he staggered from the bed and turned the key in the lock.

'What is it, sir?' asked Binger anxiously as he came in, followed by the two Kessicks.

'Light the lamp and get me a drink!' gasped Tony.

The old man obeyed and Binger poured out some water.

'Was it — was it the face, sir?' quavered Albert in a hoarse whisper.

'It was!' said Tony with a shiver. 'I owe you an apology, Albert. I laughed at your story, but it's true. It was beastly! Horrible!'

'You want a good stiff whisky!' said Binger, and left them.

'They call it the death mask,' muttered old Kessick. 'The last that seen it went queer in the 'ead, so its said. I was but a kid then, but I 'eard tell of it, though I never thought it was true.'

'It's true enough,' declared Tony. 'I emptied my gun at it, but it made no difference.'

Binger returned with half a tumbler of neat whisky, and he gulped it down gratefully. The servant remained after the others had departed, reluctant to leave his master alone.

'You're sure you wouldn't like me to stop, sir?' he asked doubtfully, when Tony suggested he should go back to bed.

'No. I'll be all right,' said Ware. 'You hop along.'

When he had persuaded Binger to go and had relocked the door he got back into bed and lay for a long time trying to find a plausible explanation for what appeared an inexplicable mystery. And he was still without a solution when he fell asleep, to be disturbed no more that night.

2

Blank cartridges

The following morning he woke early, feeling remarkably well despite his disturbed night. With the yellow sunlight streaming in through the window the room assumed a more cheerful aspect, and his previous night's fears appeared childish. One thing stuck in his mind, however, most unpleasantly. He had emptied his pistol at point blank range and the thing had merely laughed.

The thought came to him to examine the walls for marks, and getting out of bed and pulling on a dressing gown he made a search of the panelling with the utmost care, but there was not even a scratch let alone a bullet hole.

He frowned. He had fired ten shots; the bullets must have gone somewhere. He went over to the table and picked up the automatic and examining the barrel he found it choked with carbon. A great understanding began to dawn upon him. The weapon had lain on the table by the bedside all the while he had been at dinner, the entire evening for that matter — ample time for anyone to tamper with it. Evidently the bullets had been broken out, a simple enough job, and he had been firing blanks.

His mouth hardened and his eyes narrowed. This was not the work of a ghost but of a human being. But why had it been done? Who was responsible and how had the dreadful apparition come and gone?

He was whistling softly to himself when Binger put in an appearance.

'Good morning, sir,' greeted the little Cockney. 'I hope you weren't disturbed again?'

'I wasn't,' said Anthony, seizing a towel. 'While I'm having my bath, take a look at that automatic. I'd like to have your opinion when I come back.'

When he returned a few minutes later he found his servant phlegmatically brushing his clothes.

'Well, did you have a look at it?' he inquired.

'Yes, sir. You been firin' blanks, sir,' said Binger.

Tony nodded.

'Quite unintentionally,' he said. 'Some thoughtful person kindly tampered with my pistol while I was having dinner last night. No wonder that thing chuckled when I opened fire.'

Binger scratched his head without comment.

'What's got me guessing,' continued his master, as he brushed his hair, 'is how the Hell the stunt was arranged. Just a face in the air, no body, nothing!'

'It couldn't have been either of the Kessicks, sir,' said Binger, ' 'cause they came along with me.'

'No. There must be somebody in the house we don't know anything about,' asserted Tony. 'Well, I hope they'll try again, I'll be prepared for 'em next time.'

After breakfast he called Binger and suggested they should explore the neighbourhood.

'I want to refresh my memory,' he said,

as they left the drive and strode down the narrow winding path through the towering rocks. 'I haven't seen this place since I was a kid of twelve. We'll climb to that peak,' — he indicated it with a jerk of his head — 'and have a general look round.'

From the top of the lofty eminence they were able to see for miles in every direction. On the north and west the ground rose precipitously to a range of mountains, but the slope to the south was less steep and a mere cart-track, barely visible among the scrub and heather, wound down to the drive gates from the white road some three miles distant.

The house itself was built in the native stone, with a grey-slated roof, and rather austere in its architecture. A plantation of gaunt trees backed it, and an extensive but ill-kept lawn sloped away from the front. Around the whole grounds ran a stone wall about six feet high, broken only by the iron gates of the entrance.

A curiously-shaped pool of black water lay a mile to the left, in a setting of melancholy crags. Binger remarked upon it.

'Funny looking pond,' he said, pointing. 'Looks like a great big foot.'

Tony nodded.

'They call it the Devil's footprint,' he said. 'I remember it well. There's an idea in these parts that it's bottomless. By Jove, the air's fine!' He drew in great lungfuls as he gazed with shining eyes at the rather severe landscape.

'What are you going to do about tonight, sir?' Binger broke in suddenly. 'In case there's any more tricks?'

Tony took out his cigarette case and helped himself to a cigarette before replying.

'I'll tell you what I thought,' he said. 'I'll load the automatic about nine o'clock and leave it lying on the table as I did before. There's a little alcove just outside my door and if you take up your position there till bedtime you'll see if anyone tries to monkey with the bullets. How's that?'

'Sounds O.K. to me!' said the little Cockney.

'There's something very queer going on, obviously,' remarked Tony, as they began to climb down from the mass of rocks on which they had been standing, 'and I'm going to find out what it is.'

At nine o'clock that evening he put his scheme into operation. Carefully loading the automatic he left it on the table and a whispered word as he came out of the door informed him that Binger had already taken up his position. Going downstairs he whiled away the time before bed with a book

It was eleven o'clock when he shut the volume and rose. Binger was still concealed behind the curtain of the alcove when he reached his room.

'Anything happened?' he asked in a low voice.

The servant shook his bullet head.

'No, sir,' he answered. 'Not a blinkin' soul's been near.'

Tony opened the door and went in, the other following. Picking up the pistol he withdrew the clip of cartridges from the butt and his lips pursed as he saw that the bullets had been withdrawn.

'Well, that proves it!' he said grimly.

'Proves what, sir?' asked the astonished Binger.

'That there's a secret entrance of some kind to this room, answered Tony promptly. 'It's the only explanation. Load that thing up again, George, and listen to me. When everything's quiet tonight you come along to this room. I'll be waiting for you, and if our friend the death mask turns up God help him.

Binger departed and Tony rapidly undressed, put out the light and, sitting on the bed, awaited his servant's return. He slipped into the room so quietly that until he spoke his master was unaware of his presence.

''Ere I am, Gov'nor,' he whispered. 'What do we do now?'

'You slide into bed,' answered Tony. 'I'm going to take up a position over here by the window.'

The night was very still, in contrast to the previous one there was no wind, and the time dragged by slowly. The clock in the hall chimed twelve, then half-past, and both the watchers were beginning to wonder if their vigil was to be in vain.

One o'clock came sonorously from the muffled bell below. The sound had barely faded to silence when Tony became aware of the cold draught he had experienced before.

He stiffened, bracing himself for whatever might occur. In the stillness he heard a faint scraping noise, and then, with a suddenness that was startling, the face loomed out of the blackness, death-grey and horrible. But he was no longer afraid.

With his eyes fixed on the floating apparition he began to steal forward silently, his naked feet making no sound. And when he was but a yard away he sprang!

In the darkness he came upon a solid body, and his hand closed upon an arm. He lashed out into the darkness with his right and heard a strangled cry, and then something crashed down on his head and his senses merged with the blackness of the room . . .

3

The man on the rock

The room was filled with the vague light of morning when he struggled back to consciousness. He stared at the grey outlines of the oak beams above him, his mind in a chaotic whirl, his head throbbing.

A peculiar odour filled the room which he could not account for, and when, with an effort, he forced himself to a sitting posture the first thing he saw was Binger lying motionless on the bed.

Staggering to his feet he went over and stared down at the man anxiously. He saw with relief that the servant was still breathing, and going over to the window he flung wide the casement, letting in the fresh keen, moorland air. A few breaths of it and he felt better. Something white lay on the floor between the window and the bed and picking it up he became aware again of that peculiar odour. This time he recognized it.

'Ether!' he muttered,

Crossing to the washstand he splashed some water into the bowl and dipping his head into it rubbed his face briskly with a towel. By the time he had finished the operation his cure was practically completed.

Dipping a sponge into the water he went over to Binger and bathed his face and neck. Presently the man's eyes opened and he stared up at him vacantly.

'Feeling better?' asked Tony.

'Blimey!' said the Cockney huskily, 'Wot 'appened?' He made an effort to rise, but Tony pushed him gently back.

'Lie still for a bit,' he said. 'You've been drugged.'

Binger sank back on the pillow with a groan, and while he waited for him to fully recover Tony sat on the edge of the bed and thought over the events of the night.

There was now no shadow of doubt that the 'ghost' was real, worked by somebody dressed in black and wearing a mask painted with luminous paint. His expression became grim.

The trick was more than a practical joke. Nobody would carry a joke to the length of knocking out and chloroforming their victims. There was some other reason behind it, and he could only think of one; that someone was determined to drive him from the place. But for what object? Why should anybody be anxious to scare him away, and who could the someone be?

He could think of no reasonable explanation and was still searching when Binger sat up, rubbing his forehead.

'Feeling all right now?' he asked.

The servant nodded.

'I'm in the pink, except for a bit of an 'eadache,' he replied.

'Then perhaps you'll tell me what happened to you?' said Tony.

'Well, I dunno as I can,' muttered Binger, with a scowl. 'It all 'appened so quick like. I saw that there face come out o' the dark an' was just gettin' ready to lam it when somebody got me by the throat and jammed a pad over me nose and mouth.'

'Which shows that there must have been more than one of them,' grunted Tony. 'You didn't see anything of your assailant?'

Binger shook his head.

'No, I didn't, sir,' he answered. 'I was collared from be'ind some'ow.'

Tony frowned.

'Did you feel that cold draught?' he inquired.

'Yes,' said Binger. 'It was more like a blinkin' wind!'

'So did I,' said his master. 'There must be some sort of trapdoor near the bed. Let's have a look.'

They made a careful search of the entire room, but without success. If there was a secret entrance — and it seemed there must be — then the place was very carefully concealed. They gave it up at last and Tony picked up his towel.

'We might as well get dressed,' he said. 'By the way, don't say anything at all to the Kessicks. If they ask you how you slept say fine.'

'Blimey, it'll be the truth!' grunted Binger. 'I ain't slept so sound before in me natural!'

He departed for his own room, and when Tony had bathed, shaved, and dressed he went down to breakfast.

Albert was in the dining room, and although Tony watched him keenly not by so much as a twitch of an eyelid did he show that he knew anything of the night's events. He inquired civilly whether Tony had slept well and evinced no surprise on being told that he had.

Ware was puzzled. If the Kessicks knew nothing about the business who was at the bottom of the conspiracy? He tried to fathom the mystery while he ate his breakfast, but without result.

When the meal was over he lit his pipe, and spent the rest of the morning in a detailed inspection of his new property, accompanied by the curious and interested Binger.

The house was large and rambling, and in places in a bad state of repair. After tea they went for a walk on the moor, discussing the unpleasant and alarming incident of the night before, and trying to evolve a plan for dealing with any future occurrence of the same kind.

They had emerged from the clustering rocks to the open stretch of moorland when Binger suddenly touched Tony's arm.

'There's a feller up on the top of that lump of rock watchin' us through spy glasses,' he muttered. 'I spotted him five minutes ago. He's tryin' to keep 'imself 'idden.'

To their left rose a gaunt peak, and as Tony looked up at the summit he saw a sudden flash — the reflection of the setting sun on glass. It vanished as he looked and did not come again.

'Sure you weren't mistaken?' he asked.

'No!' replied Binger with conviction. 'There's a bloke spyin' on us.'

'In that case,' said Tony, 'I think we might have a look at the gentleman. I'd like to know what his game is.'

They changed their direction and walked towards the rocky mass.

'When we get underneath we shall be out of sight from the top,' said Tony. 'Then we can work round to the other side and climb up.'

It was a stiff climb, but eventually they reached the summit, and the first thing

Tony saw was a man lying at full length, a pair of field glasses to his eyes, scanning the countryside. He was lying partially in the shadow of an upstanding needle of rock, and stealthily they began to approach him.

They had got within two yards of the prone figure when it rose ponderously to its feet, calmly dusted the knees of its trousers, and remarked in a slow, sleepy voice.

'You two fellers don't know the first thin' about takin' a man by surprise.'

Tony stared at the bulky figure before him.

The watcher was a huge man with many chins and two half-closed eyes that surveyed them sleepily.

'I thought you was comin',' said this surprising individual. 'I guessed you'd seen the sun reflected on my glasses and was goin' to do a bit of investigatin' when you turned off and came in this direction. So I thought I'd wait for you. It's just as well if we get acquainted.'

Tony raised his eyebrows in astonishment.

'I don't quite understand,' he said.

'What's the idea?'

'You might say there was several,' replied the stout man. 'I'm full of ideas, Mr. Ware.'

'I'm glad to hear it,' said Tony, recovering himself. 'You seem to know me, but I'm darned it I know you.'

'We can soon put that right!' retorted the other. 'My name's Superintendent Budd. I'm from Scotland Yard.'

'From Scotland Yard?' repeated Anthony, more astonished than ever.

'Yes,' said Mr. Budd sleepily. 'It's a little buildin' on the Thames Embankment — '

'I know what Scotland Yard is!' snapped Tony. 'But why are you here? And how do you know my name?'

'News travels quickly in a place like this,' answered Mr. Budd. 'That's how I know about you, Mr. Ware. An' I'm here because — '

He stopped dead, his mouth still forming the words he had been about to utter. For at that moment a shrill scream broke the stillness of the evening — a scream followed almost instantaneously by two shots fired in rapid succession!

4

Death on the moor

Mr. Budd was the first to recover from the shock of that terror-laden scream. The sleepy look vanished from his face and his eyes opened very wide.

'There's somethin' nasty goin' on somewhere,' he muttered rapidly. 'Come on!'

He set off at a surprising speed, considering his bulk, and began scrambling down the side of the huge rock, Ware and Binger following. They reached the base of the crag and set off at a stumbling run over the boulder-strewn moorland.

'We'd better separate,' panted Mr. Budd. 'If we spread out we shall cover more ground.'

The others nodded and hurried on, peering behind the heaps of scattered rock that dotted the heather.

The stout Superintendent had just passed a hillock when there came a hail from Binger.

'Over 'ere!' he shouted. 'Come on, I've found 'im!'

He was standing by a clump of stunted bushes waving his arms, and Ware and the stout detective hurried to his side.

'This is the bloke wot screamed,' said Binger simply, and pointed to a crumpled figure that lay face downwards in the scrub.

Mr. Budd dropped on one knee and turned the silent form over on its back. As he did so Tony gave a stifled exclamation.

'Good God, Albert!' he muttered in horror.

Mr. Budd looked up quickly.

'You know this feller?' he asked.

'He's one of the servants from my place,' explained Tony.

'And that accounts for the shots,' muttered the big man, pointing to the rapidly spreading red stain on the man's grey tweed coat.

'Is he dead?' whispered Tony huskily.

Mr. Budd laid his fleshy hand on the

breast of the prostrate figure and slowly shook his head.

'No, he isn't,' he answered, 'but I don't think he's far off it.'

Even as he spoke a spasm contracted the ashen face and the man's eyes flickered over. The twisted mouth moved as though he was making a frantic effort to speak, and Mr. Budd bent his head lower in an effort to catch what the dying man said. An unintelligible mutter was all he could hear, and then two words separated themselves clear and distinct: 'Gentleman . . . he . . . '

The rest was lost in a choking gurgle — Albert was dead!

'We'll have to notify the police at once,' said Mr. Budd. 'Per'raps, sir, your man could go along to the village and find my sergeant. He'll be drinkin' lemonade in the bar of the Scarsgill Arms. Tell 'im what's happened and he'll know what to do. You can't mistake him, he's like a hop-pole, only less intelligent lookin'.'

Tony turned to Binger.

'Will you do that?' he said. 'Quick as you can.' And then, when his servant had departed: 'I seem to have dropped into the middle of a sensational novel. First ghosts and then murder — '

Mr. Budd eyed him sharply,

'What d'you mean by ghosts?' he asked, and Tony gave a brief account of his two nights at Crag Fell.

The fat detective listened, his eyes almost completely closed, and to his bewilderment evinced no surprise.

'Interestin' and peculiar,' he murmured. 'So I haven't been wastin' me time. I thought not when I heard what that feller said before he died.'

'What did he mean?' asked Tony. ''Gentleman . . . he . . . ''?'

'He was namin' his murderer,' replied Mr. Budd. 'That's what he was doin'. 'The Gentleman' killed him.'

'Who's the Gentleman?' demanded Tony.

'A devil!' answered the stout man, and his slow, lethargic voice was harsh. 'A clever, callous devil, that's what he is!'

Something in the way he spoke sent a cold shiver down Tony's spine.

'And you think he's at the bottom of all

this business round here,' he began.

'He's at the bottom of that feller's death,' interrupted Mr. Budd, seating himself on a boulder and producing a black and unpleasant looking cigar. 'Tell me, Mr. Ware, your uncle's death was an accident, wasn't it?'

Tony was a little surprised at this abrupt change of subject.

'Yes,' he answered. 'He fell over the edge of a quarry and broke his neck.'

'Who found him?' murmured the fat Superintendent, deliberately searching through his pockets for a box of matches.

'His valet,' replied Tony.

'Is he still livin' at Crag Fell — the valet I mean?' asked Mr. Budd.

'No, my uncle left him a house, a cottage at Grey Rock. He's living there, I believe. The only people at Crag Fell are myself, my man, Binger, old Peter Kessick and, until now, Albert.'

'I see,' murmured the big man.

He blew out a cloud of smoke with satisfaction and Tony waited for him to say something further. He was disappointed. He seemed quite content to sit with his eyes half closed smoking. And he was still dreamily enjoying his cigar when Binger returned, accompanied by a constable; a tall, thin man with the most lugubrious expression Tony had ever seen, and an Inspector of the local police.

The Inspector took all particulars, and with the assistance of Binger and the constable succeeded in the difficult task of removing the body of Albert by stretcher to the car, which they had been forced to leave a mile down the road.

'I'll come back with you to Crag Fell,' said Mr Budd, after he had held a few minutes' private conversation with the Inspector. 'You'd better come too Leek.'

The lugubrious man nodded.

'There's nothing I should like better,' said Tony. 'Come and have some dinner. Perhaps you'll be able to find what I failed to do — the way that ghost player got in and out of my bedroom.'

'That,' murmured Mr. Budd dreamily, 'is why I suggested comin'.'

They began to make their way back to the house, and they were turning in at the gates when the fat detective put another surprising question.

'Ever heard of a man named Wingate, Mr. Ware?' he asked.

Anthony shook his head.

'No, should I?' he replied.

'I dunno that you should,' said Mr. Budd. 'But if you haven't I think you will. Nice place you've got here,' he continued before Tony could put the question that was hovering on his lips. 'That bit of ground over there 'ud make a nice rose garden, plenty of sun and nice and sheltered.'

He launched into a long dissertation upon roses and their growth and Tony concluded that this was his hobby.

Breaking the news to old Kessick was a task that he didn't relish, but having settled the big man and his thin companion comfortably by the fire he set about tackling this unpleasant but necessary duty. The old man was terribly cut up, so much so indeed that Anthony insisted on his going to bed and resting until the effects of the shock had worn off,

'Binger can manage the cooking,' he said, and came down to acquaint his servant with the new arrangements.

Mr. Budd was staring at the leaping flames when he entered the sitting room; the lean sergeant perched uncomfortably on the edge of a chair gazing at him mournfully.

'Y'know, Mr. Ware,' said the fat man slowly, 'this is a much bigger thin' than you realize.'

'I don't realize anything, yet!' retorted Anthony.

'No, well I'm tellin' you,' went on Mr. Budd. 'It's big an' it's dangerous. The feller at the bottom of this business has tried to get you out by a trick an' he's failed. He'll try somethin' more drastic next time.

'You're referring to this man you call The Gentleman?' asked Tony.

'Yes, that's him,' Mr. Budd's eyes narrowed. 'One of the most dangerous criminals I've ever had to deal with, an' I've had a few.'

'Why is he called The Gentleman?' asked Tony curiously.

'It's a name he's got among the little crooks,' answered the other. 'He's supposed to come of a good family. Nobody

185

knows his real name or anythin' much about him.'

'What does he specialise in?' said Tony, lighting a cigarette.

'Anythin' to make a profit,' answered Mr. Budd. 'He was mixed up with three cases of blackmail and a robbery and he's dabbled in the dope traffic and is suspected of two murders.'

'Sounds a nice, pleasant sort of fellow to have about the house,' remarked Tony.

At that moment Binger came in with a heavily-laden tray which he set down on the table. When they had done full justice to the rather rough and ready meal Mr. Budd suggested they might have a look at the bedroom.

Anthony assented eagerly and, sending Binger for the lamp, accompanied the big man and his melancholy companion up the stairs. Mr. Budd looked round the gloomy room with pursed lips, and went over to the massive four-poster bed.

'Where did you feel this draught come from?' he asked.

'Somewhere near the head of the bed,' replied Tony. 'I've sounded all the panels but there's not a sign of anything.'

Mr. Budd picked up the lamp and held it close to the wall, inspecting it carefully while the other three watched him. He tested each section of the panelling and ran his fat, stubby fingers over the carving, but he found nothing.

For some minutes he stood, lamp in hand, gently massaging his fat chins, and then he walked over to a big mahogany wardrobe that stood in an angle of the wall. At each side the old wood was carved with elaborate designs in the form of cupids, and he began pulling and pressing methodically.

Nothing happened, however, until he pushed at the side of the massive piece of furniture, and then, to the watchers' astonishment, there was a sharp click and the whole wardrobe slid easily and noiselessly along, revealing an oblong gap in the floor. Peering into the dark aperture they saw that a flight of stone steps led downwards.

'That's the way your friend the ghost came,' remarked Mr. Budd softly. 'Now, I wonder where they lead?'

5

The hidden chamber

'You stay here, Leek,' he said, 'in case anyone should take us by surprise from this end, and don't go to sleep. You'd better come with me, Mr. Ware.'

'I wouldn't miss it for the world,' said Tony. 'You stay with the sergeant, Binger.'

'And if he looks like falling asleep,' added Mr. Budd, 'pinch 'im — if you can find any flesh to get hold of.'

'I'm not tired!' protested Leek dismally. 'And when 'ave I fallen asleep durin' me work?'

'I've never seen you do any!' retorted the fat detective crushingly, and began to descend the stone steps which were built in the thickness of the wall, holding the lamp above his head.

Tony followed him, and presently, after what seemed an eternity, they found themselves in a flag-paved passage. By the light of the oil lamp they saw a heavy oak door some twenty feet ahead. On reaching this barrier the big man tried his weight against it, but the door was immovable and there was no sign of a key.

Tony was about to comment on this unexpected obstacle when his companion gripped his arm and blew out the lamp, leaving them in pitch darkness.

'Listen!' he whispered.

Tony listened, and faintly, as though far away, came the sound of voices. He leaned forward to try and catch what was being said, steadying himself by resting his hand lightly on the door. As he did so his fingers came in contact with something that removed beneath his touch.

At first he wondered what it was, and then he realized. In the upper part of the door was a sliding panel. He pushed it gently aside. A faint glimmer of light appeared, and at the same moment the voices grew louder.

He looked through, drawing in his breath with a little hiss of astonishment at what he saw. He was staring into a long, low-ceilinged, cellar-like room without windows. The floor was of stone and in the centre stood a refectory table, black with age and dirt. By the left hand wall was a low couch, and the whole scene was lighted by an electric lamp that stood on the table.

On the couch, apparently asleep, lay a girl, and standing by her side was a tall figure in a soiled overcoat and cap. He had his back to the door so it was impossible to see his face. He was looking at the bound figure of a man who sat propped up in a chair in the middle of the strange apartment. His close cropped hair and unshaven chin gave him a rough, uncouth appearance, enhanced by rather bold, defiant eyes and a savage scowl.

Bending over him was an extraordinary figure, a medium-sized man whose face was concealed by a bag-like mask of black material that completely covered his head. He was speaking slowly, but though Tony could hear the sound of his voice quite plainly he couldn't distinguish a word he said.

Presently he threw up his hands in an extravagant gesture of anger. The bound man rasped out a few words in a voice that was husky with fury — or fear. The masked man listened for perhaps three seconds, then he leaned forward and struck the other full on the mouth.

The watchers saw a thin trickle of blood run down the bound man's unshaven chin, and it was only by a supreme effort that Tony kept silent.

'I'm not going to — ' he began in a fierce whisper, and stopped as an elbow dug into his wrist.

'Shut up!' said Mr. Budd, and Tony felt him stoop and fumble in the region of the lock.

He applied his eye once more to the grille. The man in the chair had taken the blow without flinching and with a shrug of the shoulders the hooded man walked across to the sleeping girl.

Tony, repressing his anger with difficulty, watched what followed. He saw the masked man bend over the girl and a glint of light showed on some metal object in his hand which he waved towards the bound man in the chair. The prisoner strained violently at his bonds and his eyes grew anxious and full of horror.

The hand holding the metal object — Tony saw that it was a hypodermic syringe — came slowly down towards the inert figure of the girl — nearer — nearer.

It had almost reached her cheek when he jumped violently as there came a deafening report from beside him.

'My God, what's that?' he cried.

'I've shot out the lock!' snarled Mr. Budd, and flung the door open.

The masked man swung towards them, and his hands dropped to his pocket.

'I want you — ' began the detective, but the other shot from his pocket, and Tony felt the wind of the bullet as it hummed viciously past his ear.

At the same instant the man in the coat and cap sprang forward and swept the light from the table, plunging the place in darkness. Mr. Budd muttered an oath below his breath. He dare not shoot now for fear of hitting the man in the chair.

'Put up your hands!' he said, trying to bluff, and was answered by a fusillade of shots that whistled round them and smacked viciously into the door. They heard a scuffling sound in the darkness, followed by a thud and then, suddenly, a pungent, suffocating odour caught them by the throat and set them choking and coughing.

Mr. Budd recognised it instantly, and gave warning of the danger.

'Get back, Mr. Ware!' he gasped. 'It's chlorine gas!'

The deadly vapour was rapidly filling the chamber and they leaped for the door by which they had entered, stumbled through and pulled it shut behind them. In the pitch-darkness they felt their way back along the passage, up the stairs, and finally emerged from the oblong hole in the floor of the bedroom.

There was no sign of Binger or the melancholy sergeant. Tony uttered an exclamation of surprise.

'Where are they — ' he began, and received his answer as a figure staggered through the door towards them, swaying dizzily. 'Binger!' cried Tony, as he recognised the man. 'What's the matter, are you hurt?'

The only answer was a faint moan, and then Binger collapsed almost at his feet.

Mr. Budd struck a light and applied it to a candle on the table by the bed.

'What's happened to him?' he muttered, and drew in his breath sharply as he saw that the motionless man's coat was wet with blood!

6

The man who was bound

'He's still breathin',' said Mr. Budd, after a brief examination. 'Help me get him on the bed, and then find another lamp, will you?'

Tony assisted him to lay the wounded man on the bed, and went downstairs. When he came back with a lamp he found that the fat detective had stripped off the man's coat and opened his shirt, revealing a nasty gash on his right side. He had been stabbed, but the knife, luckily, had glanced off a rib and only inflicted a flesh wound, which the big man soon had washed and bandaged.

When Tony, who had gone to get him some whisky at the Superintendent's suggestion, returned, he was coming round.

'Here, drink this,' said Mr. Budd kindly, as Binger opened his eyes, 'and then tell us what happened.'

The little Cockney gulped down the neat spirit.

'Do a flop, did I?' he said a little weakly. 'It ain't like me to throw a dummy at a scratch.'

'Anyone 'ud faint from the amount of blood you've lost,' murmured the fat detective. 'Now, what's happened to my sergeant?'

'Well,' began Binger, 'it was like this. I was standin' by the winder talkin' to your feller when all of a sudden I sees a flash of light by the wall near the stable. Hello, I says, there's somethin' funny goin' on out there. He thought it was funny, too, so we went downstairs and made our way out to the place where I had last seen the glim. There was somebody about and we was searchin' for them, an' all at once I 'eard people movin' in the wood like a 'erd of elephants. I was runnin' towards the noise when some cove tripped me up and shoved a knife in me ribs. I don' know exactly what happened after that, but I thought I'd better get back 'ere, an' that's all I remember.'

'H'm!' said Mr. Budd, his brows drawn together. 'And what happened to Leek?'

'I dunno what 'appened to 'im,' said Binger. 'Ain't 'e come back?'

The stout man shook his head.

'No,' he began seriously, and stopped as there came a stumbling step from below.

Tony stepped quickly to the door and in the light from the hall saw the lean figure of Sergeant Leek slowly mounting the stairs.

'We was just wonderin',' said Mr. Budd as his subordinate entered, 'what had happened to you.'

'I fell into an 'ole!' said Leek with an injured expression, and they saw that his clothes were smeared with mud and slime. 'I fell into an 'ole and it knocked all the breath out of me body.'

'You're always fallin' into somethin',' grunted Mr. Budd unkindly. 'While you go floppin' about like a performin' seal all sorts of thin's have 'appened.'

'I couldn't 'elp it!' protested the sergeant mournfully. 'It was dark and I didn't see the 'ole until I was in it. What's been 'appenin'?'

'Oh, nothin',' said Mr. Budd sarcastically. 'Mr. Ware and I have nearly been gassed and this poor feller here as had a knife stuck in his ribs, but except for that it's been very quiet!'

'What did you find down there?' asked Binger, as the sergeant stuttered incoherently to defend himself.

Tony explained briefly.

'Blimey!' exclaimed Binger. 'It's a rum go ain't it? Who d'you think the feller in the chair was?'

'The feller in the chair,' interposed Mr. Budd: sleepily, 'was an escaped convict. His name's Wingate, and he escaped from Princetown prison five days ago.'

Tony looked at him in astonishment.

'What on earth is he doing here?' he demanded.

The fat man shrugged his broad shoulders.

'I'm as much in the dark as you are,' he replied. 'But there's one thing that sticks out a mile, and that is that they were tryin' to get some kind of information out of Wingate.'

'That's how it looked to me,' agreed

Tony. 'But what information were they after, and who was the girl that masked devil was threatening with the hypodermic?'

Mr. Budd extracted a cigar from his waistcoat pocket and looked at it critically.

'If I was a guesser,' he said, 'I should guess the girl to be Wingate's daughter. The gentleman was obviously going to do somethin' to her in order to force Wingate to talk.'

'Then for Heaven's sake let's do something,' said Tony impatiently, 'instead of standing here talking!'

'What do you suggest we should do, Mr. Ware?' asked Mr. Budd, piercing the end of his cigar with his thumbnail. 'We can't go after 'em in the dark.'

'What's your idea then!' snapped Tony.

'My idea,' answered the detective slowly, 'is to wait until that gas has dispersed and then I'm goin' to have a look at that room below. That, I think 'ull be all for tonight. Tomorrow mornin' I shall have a word or two with your uncle's valet.'

Tony stared at him.

'What the deuce for?' he asked frankly.

'He can't have anything to do with this business.'

'Did I say he had?' inquired Mr. Budd gently. 'And perhaps you can tell me, Mr. Ware, what you mean by 'this business'?'

'Well, everything,' said Tony.

'Everythin'!' repeated the big man. But we don't know everythin', so a few words with the valet won't do any harm. What's his name, by the way?'

'Deeks,' said Tony. 'I don't know what you hope to gain by seeing him.'

'Maybe I was born curious,' murmured Mr. Budd, dipping the end of his cigar into the candle flame. 'Maybe I've got a hunch. There's a lot of things I'd like to have an explanation for. Let's see what we do know,' he continued thoughtfully. 'One: This feller Wingate was servin' a sentence for murder. He wasn't hanged because the jury disagreed. Five days ago he escaped from prison with outside assistance and is brought by this Gentleman feller, who isn't so gentlemanly in 'is habits, to a secret chamber in this house, with the evident intention of being forced to divulge some information which our

Gentleman friend wants to know. Two: Your uncle falls into a quarry and breaks his neck. Three; You inherit your uncle's estate and come to take up your residence in this house. Four; The Gentleman — I think we can safely conclude he's responsible — tries to scare you out of it. Five: A feller called Albert, son of an old servant of your family, is shot on the moor. Before he dies he names, or tries to name, The Gentleman as his murderer. Those are the bits I want to stick together.'

'But my uncle's death was accidental — ' began Tony.

'Maybe it was,' said Mr. Budd thoughtfully, 'and maybe it wasn't. I've learnt never to take anythin' for granted, Mr. Ware. Your uncle fell over a quarry and broke his neck. His death was attributed to an accident, but that doesn't say it was an accident.'

'Are you suggesting he was murdered?' demanded Tony.

'No, no!' The fat man shook his head. 'I'm not suggestin' anythin', but I'd like a word with that valet all the same.' He turned and glanced at the oblong hole in the floor. 'I should think by now,' he said, 'that the gas has cleared off. Suppose we go and have another look at that underground room?'

'Shall I come?' asked Sergeant Leek mournfully.

Mr. Budd sniffed.

'No, you go and clean yourself,' he answered. 'You're in a disgusting state and you smell horrible! If you come we'll all be gassed over again.'

He picked up the candle and began to descend the steps, Tony following him. There was still a faint smell of chlorine, but the air was breathable. They found the oil lamp near the door and Mr. Budd lit it.

Inside the low ceilinged chamber beyond the door the acrid smell of the gas was stronger. The fat man looked about him and pointed to another door facing the one by which they had entered.

'That's the way he escaped,' he murmured. 'We'll have a look and see where it leads to.'

He went over to the exit, opened it, and

passed through with Tony at his heels. On the other side was a short passage, and then a similar flight of steps as the one leading from the bedroom which ran upwards into the darkness.

Mr. Budd mounted carefully and presently came to a circular wooden ceiling, which rested on brickwork. He pushed at this and it opened, falling back with a thud. With his head projecting through the aperture the fat man looked about him. He saw that he had emerged in the middle of a thick clump of bushes that effectively concealed the entrance to the steps. He scrambled out and found that he was standing in dense shrubbery near the stables.

'Nobody 'ud dream there was a trap door in the middle of this,' he said to Tony when the latter joined him. 'Unless you knew it was there you'd never find the place. It looks to me as though it had been a well, or somethin' of the sort at one time. Come along, we'll go back and see if there's anythin' to be found below.'

They retraced their steps to the underground room and Mr. Budd handed the lamp to his companion.

'Hold this, will you, Mr. Ware,' he said, 'and I'll run over the place on the chance there may be somethin' interestin'.'

With Tony following him with the lamp he made a quick but thorough search of the place. At the end of fifteen minutes he had satisfied himself that there was nothing.

'We'll go back now,' he said, as he straightened up with a yawn. 'And I think a drop of that whisky you've got 'ull be very acceptable.'

They came back to the bedroom a few minutes later, and closing the secret entrance the Superintendent wedged the bed, with Tony's help, against the wardrobe so that it was impossible to open it.

'That'll guard against a possible surprise visit,' he remarked. 'And now I think, as a matter of precaution, we'll have a look through the rest of the house.'

Sergeant Leek, more or less presentable, appeared at that moment and the three of them searched the place from top to bottom, but there was nobody concealed anywhere. When this had been completed, they carried the wounded Binger to his own room, and, dog-tired, they made their way to the dining room. Tony poured out two stiff drinks, gave one to Mr. Budd and handed the other to Leek.

The sergeant shook his thin head.

'No, thank you, sir,' he said. 'I never touch anything alcoholic.'

'If you did you might look a little more cheerful,' said Mr. Budd. 'Why you ever entered the police force at all beats me. You'd 'ave made a grand undertaker.'

He gulped his drink and set down the empty glass.

'Well, I think we'd better be going, Mr. Ware,' he said. 'It's a fair way to Scarsgill and I want to be up early in the mornin'.'

'Why not stay here?' suggested Tony. 'There's plenty of room.'

Mr. Budd considered this offer.

'That's very kind of you,' he said after a pause. 'I think, as a matter of fact, it 'ud be better all round.'

'Then we'll have another drink and go to bed,' said Tony, 'and I hope we shan't be disturbed during the night.'

7

The warehouse

The big car purred rhythmically along the white road crossing the moor, its headlights cutting two sword-blades of white through the darkness. It was a large saloon Rolls, its occupants consisting of three people, a liveried chauffeur, a man and a girl. The girl was evidently ill, for she lay back in a corner of the wide seat with closed eyes and her face was drawn and haggard. The man who sat in the other corner seemed very little interested in her condition and spent most of his time staring out of the window. He was well dressed in a heavy grey overcoat and soft hat and his red, rather fleshy face suggested a fondness for the good things of life, although, judging from his carefully manicured hands, he did nothing in the way of manual labour to obtain them.

The car ran smoothly on, through

Scarsgill and on to Settle, towards the London Road. On through the darkness of the night it sped, past sleeping towns and villages, until, when the morning was well advanced, it drew up before a pair of high wooden gates in a narrow ill-lighted street in Lambeth.

The chauffeur got down stiffly from his seat and stretched himself to ease the cramp induced by his long drive, Going up to the wooden gates he unlocked the padlock with a key which he took from his pocket. Returning to the car he once more took his place behind the wheel and drove it into a courtyard beyond.

Shutting off the engine he went back and closed and barred the entrance. By the time he had done this the red-faced man had descended from the back seat and was waiting for him, standing by the side of the car.

'I'm glad that's over,' he grunted. 'I'm cold and hungry,'

'So am I,' said the chauffeur. 'Wonder 'ow the other's feeling?'

The red-faced man chuckled unpleasantly.

'So long as he's still alive that's all that

matters, he replied.

'We'd better get him out as soon as possible, said the chauffeur. ''Ere, you take the girl while I look after Wingate.'

The red-faced man nodded, and crossing to a narrow door at the side of the building he unlocked it and stepped into a barn-like room stacked with bags that appeared to be filled with cement. Switching on a single dirty electric light globe he went over to a corner and began to move several of the sacks until he had cleared a space about a yard square against the wall. Stooping he pulled up one of the stone slabs with which the place was paved and tugged at an iron ring. There was a slight grating sound and the wall he had cleared opened inwards, revealing a flight of grimy steps leading downwards. He felt about inside the aperture, found the switch he sought and pressed it down. A faint light sprang up from somewhere below and he went back to the car.

The chauffeur had, in the meanwhile, lifted out the girl and propped her up on the running board and was engaged in pulling vigorously at the back of the seat.

'Give me a 'and 'ere,' he said savagely. 'The blinkin' thing's stuck!'

The red-faced man lent his assistance and between them they succeeded in sliding the entire seat, padding and all, from the groove in which it had rested. A box-like compartment was revealed and huddled in this was the figure of a man.

'I 'ope he ain't snuffed it,' muttered the chauffeur. 'There was plenty of air-'oles, so he ought to be all right.'

They got the unconscious man out and carried him into the building and down the steps, along a dimly-lighted passage and into a vaulted, cellar-like chamber supported on mouldering arches. It had the appearance of a crypt, and indeed, in years gone by a church had stood on the site of the warehouse above.

The two men deposited their burden on the stone floor and the chauffeur went over and unlocked two doors that stood side by side in a recess. They opened into small, stone cells, roughly seven feet square, windowless, dark, and smelling damp and cold.

'We'll lock this feller up first,' grunted the driver, 'and then fetch the girl.'

They bundled the still unconscious figure of their prisoner into one of the cell-like rooms, closed the heavy oak door and locked it. Retracing their steps they repeated the same operation with the girl.

'Well, that's that!' remarked the red-faced man when they were once more back in the warehouse. 'What's the next move?'

'The next move is a drink,' said the chauffeur, lighting a cigarette.

He went to a cupboard and came back with a bottle of whisky and two glasses. Splashing some of the spirit into one of them he handed it to his companion, repeated the operation with the other and swallowed the neat whisky at a draught.

'That's better!' he exclaimed with intense satisfaction. 'Now then, I'll drive you to your flat.'

'What are those two going to do about food?' said the other, gulping his drink with enjoyment.

The chauffeur shrugged his shoulders.

'I've carried out all the instructions I

was given,' he said. 'Nothin' was said about food.'

'But they'll starve — ' began the red-faced man.

'Don't go worryin' about them!' snarled the other. 'The Boss knows what he's about. I'm expectin' to 'ear from 'im durin' the day. Come on, let's get out of 'ere, I'm hungry.'

They closed the entrance to the steps leading to the vault, carefully replaced the sacks of cement as they had found them, and went out to the car. The sun was flooding the pavements with yellow as the big machine turned out of the narrow street and headed towards the West End.

8

The valet

Mr. Budd came down to breakfast to find Anthony Ware already sitting before the fire, and Kessick laying the table. The old man quavered a whispered 'Good morning,' and as he left the room Tony pursed his lips.

'Poor old chap!' he said. 'I think his son's death has shaken him up pretty badly.'

'Must have been a nasty shock!' agreed Mr. Budd. 'How's your servant this morning, Mr. Ware?'

'He's got a slight temperature,' replied Tony. 'Nothing serious though. He wanted to get up, but I insisted that he should stay where he was.'

'Best thing he can do,' grunted the fat man. 'Where's my sergeant? If nobody's called him he'll go on sleepin' till next week. That feller's capacity for sleep is beyond human understandin'.'

This libellous statement was refuted by the arrival of the melancholy Leek.

'You've got some wonderful beds in this house, sir,' he remarked lugubriously. 'I don't think I've ever slept so sound.'

'We'll have some transported to Scotland Yard!' said Mr. Budd. 'And you won't have to move then for the rest of your life!'

Old Kessick came in with a tray containing bacon and eggs, toast and marmalade, which prevented the sergeant replying. When they had done full justice to the meal the big man suggested they should pay a visit to the valet, Deeks.

Tony obtained a description of the house and directions for finding it from Kessick and they set off in the clear morning air for Grey Rock. They passed a collection of cottages and farms that formed the tiny village and presently halted before the gate of a more pretentious building of the all-prevailing stone, nearly a mile from any other dwelling.

It was a quaint house, shaped like a squat T and stood well back from the narrow road, surrounded by a large, unkempt garden that was choked with weeds and rubbish. Front and back the open moor rolled away to the sky line and on each side a small clump of stunted trees offered some little protection.

'Pretty lonely place to live in,' remarked Mr. Budd, as he opened the gate. 'It don't look to me as if this feller was much interested in his surroundings or he wouldn't have let the garden get in such a state.'

He walked up the flagged path towards the porch, his sleepy eyes surveying with disapproval the evidence of neglect. The paintwork of the front door was blistered and weather-worn and the iron knocker red with rust. Queer, he thought, that a man should let his house get into such a dilapidated state.

He raised his hand and knocked sharply and the echoes of his knock had hardly died away when there came the sound of quick steps from within and the door was opened abruptly.

The man who appeared on the threshold was in direct contrast to what one would have expected from the general appearance of the place. Below medium height he was thin and dark, dressed with a neatness that almost amounted to foppishness. His hair was so smoothed and oiled that it might have been painted on his egg-shaped head, and the small black moustache, which stood out like a smudge against the sallowness of his skin was waxed meticulously.

He looked at the visitors expectantly with a pair of button-like black eyes.

'Yes?' he said a little ungraciously.

'You're Mr. Deeks, aren't you?' asked the fat detective, and the neat little man nodded.

'That's my name,' he said.

'This is Mr. Ware,' went on the Superintendent. 'The nephew of your late employer. My name is Budd and I'm a Superintendent of the C.I.D. I'd like a word with you.'

Deeks hesitated and the watchful Mr. Budd was convinced that at the mention of his name a momentary expression of fear and dismay had flashed to the small eyes. It was gone in a second, however. The man opened the door wide.

'Please come in,' he said. 'It is a pleasure to meet you, sir.' He bowed to Anthony, and shutting the door led the way to a room on the right of a square small hall.

Here another surprise awaited them. The room was dirty in the extreme. Deeks must have noticed the effect it had for he hastened to explain the reason for the neglected condition.

'I'm afraid you'll find the house rather in a bad state, sir,' he said apologetically, addressing himself to Tony. 'You see, although your uncle very generously left it to me in his will I find its situation a little too lonely for my comfort. So I have accepted a position in London.

'You'll be leavin' here then?' said Mr. Budd.

'Yes, sir,' answered Deeks. 'I'm leaving the day after tomorrow. I hope to be able to sell the house eventually. What did you wish to see me about, sir?'

'I'm hopin',' said the stout man, 'that you can give us a little information regardin' your late employer. We're tryin' to discover if there's anythin' in the late

Mr. Ware's past life which may throw a light on certain peculiar happenin's that have been goin' on at Crag Fell durin' the past few days.'

He gave the man a brief account of the efforts to scare Tony away and the shooting of Albert.

At the end of his recital Deeks shook his head in perplexity.

'I'm afraid I can't help you at all, sir,' he declared. 'I know absolutely nothing that would account for what you have mentioned.'

'D'you know whether your late master was acquainted with a man called Wingate?' inquired Mr. Budd.

'No, sir,' said Deeks. 'I never heard him speak of such a person.'

'H'm!' The fat detective rubbed his nose. 'Did you know about this secret room beneath the house?'

'No, sir,' said the valet.

'The elder Mr. Ware died rather suddenly, didn't he?' continued Mr. Budd.

'Yes, sir, it was very tragic,' replied Deeks. 'He fell into a stone quarry and broke his neck.'

The stout man put several additional questions, mostly irrelevant, they appeared to Tony, and then they rose to take their leave.

'By the way, Mr. Deeks,' said the big man, as they came out to the front door. 'Did you act as chauffeur as well as valet for the late Mr. Ware?'

The man looked slightly surprised.

'No, sir,' he answered. 'He didn't keep a car, sir.'

'Could you have driven one if he had?' asked

Mr. Budd, gazing sleepily at a straggling bush.

The valet shook his head.

'No, sir,' he replied. 'I don't understand them.'

Mr. Budd screwed up his big face.

'Drivin's a useful accomplishment in these times,' he remarked. 'Well, we'll be gettin' along. I'm sorry we disturbed you. Good mornin'.'

Deeks bowed and stood by the front door watching them as they walked down the path.

'That seems to have been a waste of

time,' remarked Tony, as they turned in the direction of Grey Rock. 'I didn't think he knew anything.'

Mr. Budd produced one of his black cigars and pierced the end with great deliberation before he replied.

'You're quite wrong, Mr. Ware,' he murmured. 'He knows everythin' and he's helped us quite a lot. He never stopped lyin', and when a man lies he's got somethin' to hide.'

Tony was surprised and showed it.

'He struck me as being remarkably open and innocent,' he said.

'Too innocent,' grunted Mr. Budd. 'D'you remember my askin' him if he drove a car, and he said no?'

'Yes,' said Anthony. 'I rather wondered what you were getting at?'

'I was gettin' at this,' said the fat detective. 'A car stopped recently at the gate of his cottage. Now, who round here would be likely to call on him in a car?'

'Possibly some tradesman's van,' suggested Tony, but the big man shook his head.

'It wasn't any tradesman's van,' he

declared. 'It was a private car, and a big one at that.'

'It doesn't seem to me to be altogether conclusive,' said Tony. 'Because a car stopped outside his gate it doesn't say he can drive one.'

'No, it doesn't,' agreed Mr. Budd, 'but his shoes do. If you'd looked at his shoes, Mr. Ware, you'd have seen that the left one showed the mark of a clutch pedal.'

'Well, you may be right.' Anthony frowned. 'I wouldn't like to argue with you, you've had more experience of these things than I have. Supposing Deeks is mixed up in this business, what are you going to do?'

'I'm goin' back with you to lunch,' said Mr. Budd, 'and then I'm goin' to find when the next tram leaves for London.'

'London?' echoed Tony.

'Yes,' nodded the big man. 'There are several things I want to find out which I can't up here.'

'But what about Deeks?' demanded Anthony.

'Surely if your suspicions are correct he ought to be watched.'

'I'm going to leave Leek to attend to that,' broke in Mr. Budd. 'He may have his limitations, but as a watcher there's no one to beat him.'

The melancholy sergeant brightened at this compliment.

'So long as the feller he's watchin',' continued the stout man, 'rings bells where ever he goes so as to keep him awake, otherwise he's liable to fall into a doze.'

He relapsed into silence and did not speak again until they reached Crag Fell.

During lunch Tony put a suggestion that he had been turning over in his mind, and Mr. Budd seemed to view it favourably.

'There's no reason why you shouldn't come up to London with me,' he said when Tony put his request.

'In fact it may prove quite useful.'

There was a train at two-thirty and they decided to catch it.

'Now,' said Mr. Budd to Leek as they took their departure, 'your job is to keep an eye on this feller Deeks, but without lettin' him know you're doin' so. You'd better find some place where you can keep the cottage under observation without bein' seen. If he goes out follow him and see where he goes. I've got it in my mind that after our visit he'll try and get in touch with our Gentleman friend.'

'Supposin' he does,' muttered the sergeant, 'what do I do then?'

'You send me a wire, or better still put through a trunk call to the Yard,' answered the big man. 'I'd say use your own intelligence if such a thing was possible, but as it isn't just try not to be more idiotic than you can help.'

Tony had arranged for Kessick to drive them to Scarsgill and a few minutes later they were seated in the local train on the way to the junction where they changed to the main line.

As they caught their last view of the melancholy moor rising in the distance like a petrified grey sea they neither of them had any premonition of the adventures that were to befall them before the last grim act of the drama in which they were both involved was played out on that wide and desolate expanse.

9

Leek's vigil

Sergeant Leek, left to himself after their departure began to make preparations for his expedition. His long face was set in an expression of abject misery for he had no relish for the task that had been assigned to him.

The thought of spending several hours on the cold and inhospitable moor was not inviting. But, he reflected gloomily, it was part of his job and there was no use kicking.

He was a little resentful that he seemed always to fall in for the most uncomfortable tasks, but that was the luck of a subordinate.

Before he left the house he paid a visit to Binger.

'I'm goin' now,' he announced mournfully, 'and I may be a long time, but don't you get worried.'

'I shan't worry, old cock!' said Binger cheerfully. 'I'm quite comfortable here.'

He looked it, propped up in his bed amongst the pillows with cigarettes and a book by his side, and Leek sighed.

'You look 'appy enough,' he remarked enviously. 'Well, you can think of me out on the cold moor doin' me duty.'

'Righto!' said Binger with a grin. 'I will. The contrast 'ull make me feel all the warmer!'

The sergeant left him and the house reluctantly and set out for Grey Rock, he had no difficulty in finding his way, and quickly discovered a convenient place from whence he could keep Deeks' cottage in full view without being seen.

Resignedly he settled down, prepared for a long and tedious vigil. Gradually the dusky shadows of the evening began to settle over the moorland, and in spite of his heavy overcoat Leek shivered, for a chill wind had sprung up and was blowing fitfully in whining gusts across the open space.

So far nothing had happened to reward his vigilance. When darkness fell a lamp was lighted in the front room, but no other sign of life showed in the cottage. Except for that star-point of light it might have been an empty house.

Another hour dragged slowly by. Leek shifted his position to ease his limbs, which were getting cramped. The darkness was intense and the night very still. Occasionally a bell from some village church tolled the hour or a railway whistle shrieked mournfully, otherwise there was nothing to break the monotony.

Another hour — two — passed more slowly than the sergeant could have believed possible.

He began to feel an overpowering desire to sleep, and he was nodding when suddenly he heard the click of a latch and the soft thud of a closing door. He jerked up his head with a start. Deeks was going out.

There came the soft clink of boots on stone and then the squeak of the gate hinge. Leek rose and moved forward. He mustn't miss him now he had gone out, but the blackness of the night made seeing impossible without getting dangerously close.

The only thing to do was to trust to sound.

The footsteps were clearly audible; stumbling, hurried steps, as though the man knew where he was going and walked rapidly.

Keeping to the grass that bordered the narrow roadway Leek followed. Firmly and without hesitation the footsteps in front went on, through the village and up the slope beyond to the open moor again.

Luckily the man he was following kept to the road, otherwise without those footsteps to guide him Leek would have lost all track.

Suddenly they stopped. Straining his eyes to pierce the darkness the sergeant made out the dim outlines of a building just ahead. He stiffened as from somewhere; out of the blackness came the sound of tapping — three short taps and then a pause — a single tap and then three more.

The man he was following was rapping on a wooden door with his knuckles.

Motionless and scarcely daring to breathe Leek waited, blinking to try and pierce the darkness. He heard the rusty rattle of bolts and then the soft whispering of voices. A wedge of light gleamed for a second, went out, the voices ceased and again came the harsh grating of bolts.

He began to creep stealthily towards where he had seen the light, and presently he came to a gate where he paused, considering what he should do next. Should he make his way back to the village and phone the Yard or should he try and find out, if possible, what was going inside the house at which Deeks had called?

He decided at length to try and learn a little more, and opening the gate, softly, slipped through, tiptoeing up to the house. The fact that there was not a glimmer of light to be seen from the front indicated one of two things — either the windows were heavily curtained or the occupied room was somewhere at the back.

He listened in the hope of distinguishing the murmur of voices, but there was no sound. He made up his mind to try the back. Cautiously he felt his way along the wall, moving slowly and warily until he came to an angle, and turning the comer stumbled on a window. Peering he found himself looking into an ordinary cottage parlour lit by a large oil lamp that stood on the table in the centre of the room.

By the side of this table stood the valet, talking earnestly to a man who was seated facing him, a black clad figure, the face and head concealed by a mask of silk — The Gentleman!

Leek pressed his ear against the pane and listened.

10

The face at the window

There was no suspicion in the valet's mind that he was being followed when he left his cottage and proceeded to walk swiftly towards Grey Rock and the lonely little house that stood a mile and a half beyond. He was too occupied with other things.

The visit that morning of Anthony Ware and Mr. Budd had given him a shock, although he congratulated himself that he had carried off the interview extremely well. It had been a trying ordeal, however, and he was anxious to report the matter as soon as possible. Anyway, the business was nearly over. Once they could persuade Wingate to speak, the stake for which he had risked his neck would soon be his, and then he could shake the dust of England from his feet forever and, take up his abode in some country where life offered more alluring possibilities.

It was a pity that so large a share would have to go to The Gentleman, but then, without his assistance he couldn't have managed the business at all. There was always the possibility that at the last moment he might be able to secure the lot for himself. Deeks had no scruples. Quite a lot of things could happen in the middle of that great tract of moorland, the wide expanse that held the secret they were trying to force Wingate to divulge.

They had one half, Wingate at the moment held the other.

His thoughts were quite pleasant as he reached his objective and raising his clenched fist he gave the usual signal with his bare knuckles on the door. There was a pause and then the door opened and an electric torch flashed blindingly in his face.

'What d'you want?' said a cold, hard voice — a voice that was cultured despite its hardness.

'Just a word with you,' muttered the ex-valet. 'Something's happened which I think you ought to know.'

'Come in,' said the voice, and the torch went out.

Deeks stepped across the threshold into pitch darkness. The door closed behind him and the bolts rattled into place. Then a hand gripped his arm and conducted him along a short passage and into a small, uncomfortably furnished room, lit by a large oil lamp on the centre of the table.

'Now, out with it! What's happened?' said the cold voice of the man who had admitted him, and the eyes under the silk mask regarded him steadily.

'That fellow from Scotland Yard, Budd, called on me this morning,' said Deeks.

'What did he want?' The words were rapped out sharply.

'He asked a lot of questions,' answered the valet. 'He wanted to know if I knew anything of the secret chamber under Crag Fell, and if old Ware and Wingate had known each other.'

The Gentleman uttered a smothered oath.

'How did he get on to that?' he

muttered. 'How much does he know?'

'I don't think he knows anything — ' began Deeks, but the other interrupted him.

'What you think doesn't matter!' he snarled. 'That fat fool must know something or he wouldn't have come nosing down here at all. Lucky I managed to get Wingate and the girl away last night.'

'Have they gone?' asked Deeks.

'Yes, Martin and Kirk took them up to the warehouse by car,' answered the masked man. 'It was too risky keeping them here.' He banged his fist down on the table in an excess of anger that made the lamp jump and flicker. 'If that fool Albert had only carried out his orders instead of getting squeamish all this trouble would have been avoided. A few drops of the stuff I gave him in Ware's coffee would have put that interfering young cub out of the way, and that infernal servant of his as well. That's what he was told to do when the ghost business didn't work. However, he won't blunder again.'

Deeks shivered.

'Was that absolutely necessary?' he whispered.

'If it hadn't been it wouldn't have been done!' retorted The Gentleman. 'Albert was useful but he was a white-livered cur and if he'd been cornered he would have squealed. They couldn't have done much to him if he'd blown the whole gaff; he wasn't in it up to the neck like you. He had nothing to do with the killing of old Ware.'

Again Deeks shivered.

'I never meant to kill him,' he muttered. 'It was an accident. I never knew he was so near the edge of the quarry when I hit him.'

'You'd have a poor chance of proving that in a court of law,' said the other harshly, and then, after a moment's pause, 'Well, what else did you want to see me about?'

'I want to know what you're going to do now,' said Deeks bluntly. 'I want to get away. This place is getting me down.'

'It shouldn't take long now,' said the other. 'Wingate is stubborn, but I think he'll break when I've had another talk with him. The girl is a fine means of persuasion.'

He broke off and swung round as there came a sudden clatter from outside the window.

'What the Hell was that?' he snarled. 'There's somebody outside! You fool, you've been followed!'

He sprang to the window. For an instant the light that streamed out focused on a white face that faded into the darkness.

'Quick!' he shouted. 'Somebody's there! Go on, you fool. Don't stand here gaping. Get out after him!'

Deeks wheeled, and rushing out of the room dashed to the front door. As he opened it he heard a rustle of bushes and a dim shape loomed for a moment to his left. He bounded forward in pursuit.

11

Leek finds trouble

As he gazed through the window Leek's breath came quickly in his excitement. There, in front of his eyes, was the man whom Mr. Budd was trying to find — The Gentleman.

What should he do? The obvious thing was to try and find out what was going on. He shifted his position slightly in order to press his ear more closely to the window, and in doing so disaster overtook him.

He slipped, knocked against a pile of boxes and flowerpots that were stacked against the wall, and brought the whole lot clattering down with an appalling din.

Almost instantly, before he had recovered his balance, the masked man appeared at the window and stared out. A stream of light focused full on his face and he heard the man inside utter a muffled exclamation.

Cursing his clumsiness Leek stumbled towards the gate, tore it open, and went racing blindly into the night. But he had been seen, for footsteps followed, getting momentarily louder and nearer! He redoubled his efforts but his feet suddenly slipped on a loose stone and before he could recover he was sprawling on his face.

The figure of his pursuer loomed out of the darkness and even as he was trying to scramble to his feet hands grasped him roughly by the arm and twisted it behind his back with a jerk that almost broke it.

The sergeant lashed out with his free hand but his assailant dodged the blow, and drawing something from his pocket he brought it sharply down on the back of his head. With a half suppressed groan Leek slipped limply to the ground and his senses fled . . .

Deeks repocketed the revolver that he had used as a 'cosh' and bending down picked up the inert form of his victim and staggered back towards the cottage.

'I caught him, anyway,' he grunted

breathlessly as he entered the sitting room and deposited his burden roughly on the floor.

'Who is it?' said The Gentleman, coming forward. 'Why, this is Sergeant Leek. He must have followed you here.'

Deeks' expression was a mixture of alarm and surprise.

'I saw no one,' he muttered.

'You would if you'd used your eyes!' snapped the other. 'This fellow's been spying on us. That fat busy body must have suspected something.' A sudden thought struck him. 'I wonder if he's anywhere round as well? We'll have to risk it, that's all.'

'What do you intend to do?' asked Deeks. He was nervous, and his nervousness showed in his twitching hands and the little pulse that had started to beat in his temple.

'Get away from here as soon as possible,' grunted the other.

He drummed impatiently on the table with his fingers for a moment and then, nodding to where Leek was lying he continued: 'You'd better tie him up. You'll find some rope in the kitchen.'

The valet opened his mouth to speak, but thought better of it, and with a muttered curse he went to look for the rope. The Gentleman's lips curved in a contemptuous smile beneath the soft silk of the mask, but it was only for a second, the next they'd set grimly and the greenish eyes were narrowed in thought.

An idea had occurred to him, an idea by which he could get rid of the cottage, the spy, and also leave no reason for anyone to wonder at his sudden disappearance from the village. He was so occupied with this scheme that he failed to see Leek's eyes open and blink for a moment.

The sergeant had returned to consciousness. He saw the tall, masked figure standing by the lamp and the whole sequence of events came flooding back to his aching brain. Without moving he lay still, closing his eyes again so that he could just see through narrow slits.

Deeks came back carrying a length of rope and began to bind his wrists and ankles. Leek allowed himself to remain limp. It was useless putting up a fight, he would stand little chance between the pair of them. The Gentleman looked round as the valet completed the task.

'Prop him up in that chair,' he ordered shortly, pointing to the chair in which he had been sitting.

Deeks gripped the sergeant by the arm and hauled him roughly to his feet. Dragging him over to the chair he bundled him into it, and he sat huddled up, his head sunk on his breast. The masked man came over and tested the cords, nodding with satisfaction.

'Now get along off home,' he said, raising his head and addressing Deeks. 'Pack your things and catch the first train in the morning to London.'

The valet stared.

'What am I to do when I get to London?' he asked sullenly.

'Go at once to Kirk,' answered the other. 'And wait at his flat until you hear from me. The address is, nine, Maudsley Gate. Now go, I've a lot to do.'

Deeks made no effort to argue, but slunk away, and a few seconds later the slamming of the front door signified that he'd gone.

For some time after the man in the mask remained motionless, thinking, then suddenly turning on his heels he left the room.

Leek raised his head and looked about him. He was feeling sick and dizzy from the blow he had received, but his brain was busy. He began to concentrate all the wits he possessed on a plan for getting out of the unpleasant situation in which he found himself. It was not so easy. A cautious test of the ropes that bound him showed that Deeks had done his work well, they refused to give a fraction of an inch. He wracked his brains. How could he get away? There was not the remotest chance of help from the outside. If he didn't return to Crag Fell, Binger would naturally become anxious, but he wouldn't even reach that stage until the morning. Both Mr. Budd and Ware had, by this time, got to London.

His thoughts broke off as he heard the sound of returning footsteps. He dropped his head back on his chest again. The

Gentleman came in, carrying a suitcase, but now his whole appearance had altered.

The mask was gone and he was dressed in tweeds, over which he wore a heavy overcoat. As he set down the bag by the table Leek saw his face and shivered inwardly. It was a cruel face, with thin, bloodless lips and slanting eyes that were almost hidden under the drooping lids. The hair was sparse and reddish-hued and grew far back on the egg-shaped head so that the smooth forehead gleamed like old, polished, ivory. The face was hairless and utterly devoid of colour and this combined with the tightness of the stretched skin gave it a horrible, deathly look that was peculiarly revolting.

Setting down the suitcase the man came over to the slumped figure of the sergeant, and after staring at him for a second suddenly stooped and jerked up his chin,

'It's useless pretending you're still unconscious,' he said. 'Unless that blow on the head killed you it's impossible for its effect to have lasted so long.'

Leek opened his eyes and stared up at the repulsive face.

'That's better!' sneered the man. 'I'm sure you'll forgive me if I take a further precaution.'

Before his prisoner could guess his intention he had whipped a handkerchief from his pocket, forced it into Leek's mouth and bound it in place with another.

'I'm afraid you'll suffer some slight inconvenience from the gag,' he remarked, 'but at least it will not be for long. They say that anticipation is better than realisation, so in order that you may test this truism yourself I will outline exactly what is in store for you.'

He paused and licked his lips.

'I'm leaving the cottage at once. At the same time I'm going to place you in a position from which you can do me no harm. It is now a little after two o'clock,' — he glanced at a gold watch on his wrist — 'Shortly before five I shall proceed to sprinkle this room rather copiously with petrol. There are two tins in the kitchen. A lighted match thrown into the room will, I think, do the rest. I only wish I'd got your fat associate here as well — but I'll get him later.' He walked over to the door. 'There are several things I've got to do,' he said from the threshold. 'Make the most of your time for it isn't very long.'

* * *

It seemed to Leek that a whole lifetime passed before the man returned, although in reality it was barely two hours. During that time he had thought of, and discarded, plan after plan. Over and over again he had tested his bonds in the forlorn hope that constant worrying would loosen them, but the more he struggled the tighter they became. He was so exhausted at last that he nearly fell out of the chair, for it was difficult enough to breathe through the gag that had been tied about his mouth, and any exertion almost choked him. His limbs cramped and numb, his head swimming and aching, he sat gazing before him despairingly. If only he could think of a plan.

The sound of approaching footsteps

drew his eyes to the door, and The Gentleman entered. He looked round quickly.

'Now, I think it is time we set the stage for the last act,' he said. 'The first thing we'll do is to put out that lamp — a premature effect would ruin everything.'

He went over and blew out the flickering flame. For an instant there was complete darkness, then the fan-shaped, white beam of an electric torch split the blackness.

'Now, as the fire must look as if it had been caused accidentally,' he muttered almost to himself, 'we must have something that could have caused it.' He knocked the lamp over and it fell with a crash to the floor, the glass and porcelain shade shattering to pieces. A large triangular portion of the chimney fell almost at Leek's feet. He saw it and caught his breath. Would his captor notice it? For in that piece of glass lay a faint chance of salvation.

He needn't have worried, for the man was now completely occupied with the preparations for the inhuman plan he had conceived. Going out into the passage he returned with two cans of petrol, and unscrewing the caps he began methodically to sprinkle the furniture, the carpet, and the wall, liberally soaking Leek's clothing and the portion of the room that immediately surrounded him.

When the last drop of spirit had been used he took the cans away.

'Now,' he remarked, returning and flashing the torch about the room. 'I think everything's ready.' He switched off the light and retreated to the door. In the darkness his voice came mockingly to Leek's ears. 'I dislike having to turn out into the cold,' he said, 'but at least I have due regard for the warmth and comfort of my guest. I always said these cottages should be supplied with central heating.'

The jeering voice ceased, then came the scraping of a match. The figure in the doorway was lit up momentarily as the match ignited and then it was shut out in a sheet of flame. The petrol-soaked carpet caught and faintly Leek heard the slamming of the front door.

Instantly he flung himself out of the

chair and rolling over on the floor began groping frantically for the triangular piece of glass. It was no easy matter, for with his hands bound behind his back he had very little play for his fingers. He found it at last, however, and getting it between the finger and thumb of his right hand he began sawing blindly at the rope round his wrists.

The fire was raging furiously licking hungrily at the walls and ceiling. He seemed to be in the middle of an inferno. The livid light lit up the doomed room, and the atmosphere grew every moment more stifling. With the perspiration streaming down his thin face Leek worked like a maniac. A hissing tongue of flame licked towards him, but the rope was giving. With all his strength he strained his wrists apart. With a sudden jerk the cords snapped. His hands were free!

His head was reeling with the heat and the fumes as he tore furiously at the bonds that secured his ankles.

His nails were torn and bleeding but he finally succeeded in loosening the knots and kicking his legs free.

Weakly he staggered to his feet and fought his way to the door through the blazing inferno. Tearing it open he reeled into the passage and pulling the gag from his mouth gulped in great gasps of fume-free air.

His brain was swimming as he groped his way to the front door and he had just sufficient strength to stagger across the threshold before the faintness came again — a great wave that engulfed him in its black depths and left him motionless and senseless, but safe, on the little path in front of the burning cottage.

12

A visit to the Yard

Mr. Budd and Anthony Ware arrived at Paddington at a late hour, and chartering a taxi outside the station were swiftly driven through the deserted streets to the Ravenscourt Hotel where Tony had elected to spend the night.

The journey had been long and tedious, but Mr. Budd refused the meal that his companion suggested.

'No, I'll be gettin' along to my little place at Streatham, if you don't mind, Mr. Ware. Per'aps you'll come round to the Yard in the morning.'

Anthony agreed, and at ten o'clock was ushered into the Superintendent's cheerless office.

'There's been nothing from Leek,' said the fat detective. 'So I suppose he's drawn a blank. Sit down, Mr. Ware. I'm expectin' a feller along in a minute who may have some news that'll interest you.'

Anthony seated himself on the single hard and uncomfortable chair that faced the desk.

'Smoke if you want to,' grunted Mr. Budd, taking out one of his inevitable black cigars and lighting it. 'It's no good givin' you one of these. I'm the only person who's ever been able to smoke 'em. They knock everybody else out in three puffs.'

A wave of the acrid smoke blew across Tony's nostrils as he finished speaking and he was quite prepared to believe him.

A knock came at the door and a thick-set, burly man entered.

'Come in, Goodly,' said Mr. Budd. 'You'll have to sit on the edge of the desk, they're mean with their furniture.'

Inspector Goodly smiled and Mr. Budd introduced Tony.

'Now,' he said, 'let's hear all you know about Wingate. You were in charge of that case, weren't you?'

The Inspector nodded.

'Yes,' he replied.

'Then let's have all the details,' grunted

the stout man, and leaning back in his chair closed his eyes.

'There aren't many,' said Goodly. 'It was one of the simplest affairs I've ever handled. The murder took place at Wingate's own house in Barchester, about eighteen months ago. The victim was a feller named Spaken — Joe Spaken. Wingate shot him in broad daylight just inside the gates of his house. A postman who was returning to the town after the morning delivery heard the shot and found Wingate bending over the dead man with a smoking pistol in his hand. He gave the alarm and Wingate was arrested. He said that Spaken had attacked him and he shot him in self-defence.

'We found afterwards, though, that Spaken had been quite friendly with him and had visited him on several occasions, Apart from that the thing that went most against him was a letter we found in Wingate's writing in the man's pocket saying that if he continued to bother him he would take steps to put a stop to it. That broke down the self-defence story, it was a definite threat.'

'Didn't he attempt to explain the letter

in any way?' murmured Mr. Budd, without opening his eyes.

Goodly nodded.

'Yes, he said that for some time Spaken had been trying to get information from him that wasn't his to give,' he answered. 'He wouldn't say what it was or discuss it at all.'

'I remember it was a peculiar case,' murmured the fat detective. 'Tell me, was this man Spaken ever known to be mixed up with The Gentleman?'

The Inspector straightened up suddenly, with a look of astonishment.

'The Gentleman?' he answered. 'Not so far as I know. Is he at the bottom of all these questions you've been asking?'

'He's certainly connected,' said Mr. Budd noncommittally. 'Was this feller Wingate acquaintance with a man named Ware?'

'Yes,' replied the Inspector without hesitation, and his sandy eyebrows rose. 'I wondered where I'd heard the name before when you introduced your friend. Yes, he was. They'd been abroad somewhere together. I know because Wingate said once that he wished that Ware had been in England at the time of his arrest.'

Mr. Budd opened his eyes.

'That's what I've been lookin' for,' he exclaimed. 'That's the link I want. A definite connection between the late Mr. Ware, The Gentleman and Wingate.'

Goodly looked from one to the other in bewilderment.

'Was Ware your uncle?' he said, letting his gaze finally rest on Tony. 'I see, that's why your name's the same. Well look here, Super, you've squeezed me dry, suppose you tell me what it's all about?'

'Not yet,' said Mr. Budd. 'I don't know what it's all about. I've only got an inkling, and I never speak till I'm sure.'

Goodly made a humorous grimace.

'He's the most exasperating fellow who ever got promotion,' he announced to Tony as he stood up. 'Well, I've got a lot of work to do if you haven't, so I'll be getting back to my office.'

When he'd gone Mr. Budd sat for a moment or two in thoughtful silence.

'H'm!' he remarked at last. 'Well, we've established a connection between your uncle and Wingate, that's somethin'.'

'We guessed that,' said Anthony.

'To guess a thing and know it for certain is a different matter,' grunted the stout Superintendent. 'Now, what we actually know about this affair is very little. We're able to say for certain that The Gentleman went to the trouble of organisin' Wingate's escape in order to force him to divulge some information that's of value — information that looks as if it concerned your uncle and Crag Fell. This mornin' we've discovered that Wingate and your uncle were friends. That gives rise to the natural assumption that this secret, or whatever it is, that The Gentleman is tryin' to force out of Wingate was shared by your uncle. What we want to discover is the nature of this secret. If necessary we shall have to go over your uncle's past life bit by bit till we find what we want, but I'm hopin' that we may obtain the same result by a shorter method.'

'How?' demanded Tony.

'By findin' Wingate,' said Mr. Budd. 'He knows the reason lyin' at the root of all this peculiar business.'

'How are you going to find him?' asked Tony dubiously. 'We don't know what happened to him after they took him out of the underground room at Crag Fell.'

'You're forgetting Deeks,' replied the fat man. 'I'm sure that he knows where Wingate is, and sooner or later he'll lead us to him.'

'That's if you're right and he's got anything to do with the affair,' said Tony.

'I'm always right!' declared Mr. Budd extravagantly. 'I never make mistakes. When he makes a move to get in touch with The Gentleman, Leek 'ull follow him and notify me at once. All we can do at the moment is to wait with as much patience as possible until we hear from him. If we don't get any news by tonight we'll go back.' He rolled his cigar from one side of his mouth to the other. 'If you've got anythin' to do in Town, Mr. Ware, you'd better do it and come back and see me here round about four o'clock.'

Anthony thought the opportunity was a good one for buying one or two things he wanted to take back with him, so he spent the rest of the day shopping. At five o'clock he returned to the Yard and found Mr. Budd sitting exactly as he had left him.

'Nothin's come yet,' said the big man. 'I'm beginnin' to think we shall have to make that return journey.'

He stopped abruptly as the shrill burr of the telephone broke in on his words. Stretching out an arm he lifted the receiver.

''Ello!' he called sleepily. 'Yes,' and then sitting up suddenly: 'Where are you speakin' from? I'll come along at once.' He scribbled something on a pad at his elbow and banged the telephone back on its rack. 'Come on,' he said, squeezing himself out of his chair and going ponderously to where his hat and coat hung on a hook behind the door. 'We're goin' to Lambeth. That was Leek and he's traced Deeks to a warehouse in Maple Street.'

He pulled open the door and went out into the corridor, followed by Tony.

'We'll call into the firearms department on our way out,' he said. 'We may need somethin' in the way of a weapon if The Gentleman's about.'

He filled up the necessary forms, collected the two pistols, handed one to Anthony, and continued on his way to the street. Here he hailed a taxi and got in after giving the driver his directions.

Maple Street proved to be a narrow, dark and unpleasant looking thorough-fare, running parallel with the river, and leaving the taxi at the top of this evil-smelling street they set off on foot.

They had covered about three hundred yards when a man detached himself from the shadows of the doorway and barred their path. It was Sergeant Leek.

'I'm glad you've got here,' he whispered mournfully. 'I'm starvin' and cold. They're both in there — Deeks and The Gentle-man.' He jerked his head at the closed gates of a courtyard on the opposite side of the street. 'Come into this alley; we can talk without being seen.'

He drew them into a narrow opening between two buildings.

'I don't want to go through the last twenty-four hours again,' he said, shaking his thin head. 'I don't suppose I'll ever be the same man again.'

'Well, that's something to be thankful for,' grunted Mr. Budd. 'It's bound to be an improvement.'

'You don't, know what I've been through,' grumbled the sergeant, and proceeded to tell them. 'The cottage was burnt to a cinder,' he concluded, and as soon as I was well enough I went along to keep an eye on Deeks. I followed him up here and he went straight to the flat The Gentleman had mentioned. He didn't stay there long, he came out after about 'alf an hour with a shortish man in chauffeur's uniform. They went to a garage nearby and got a car out. Luckily I found a taxi and followed. They went back to the flat and picked up another man, a little fat feller, and then drove down 'ere. The car's inside now.'

'In the warehouse?' asked Mr. Budd softly.

Leek nodded.

'Yes,' he answered. 'And The Gentleman went in about ten minutes ago.'

'You've done a good night's work for

once in your life,' muttered the Superintendent.

'I ought to get an Inspectorship,'
grunted Leek, 'for what I've done. Can I
go along and get somethin' to eat now?'

'Yes,' said Mr. Budd, 'you can go and
have a rest which you look as if you
needed. I'll deal with this now.'

The sergeant was moving off eagerly
when he stopped him.

'Find a call box and telephone the
Yard,' he said. 'Tell 'em to send down a
raidin' party. Tell 'em to stop at the top of
the street and I'll meet 'em there.'

Leek nodded and disappeared in the dusk.
Mr. Budd glanced across the street at the
gloomy, silent warehouse and rubbed his
hands together with satisfaction.

'We ought to get The Gentleman this
time,' he murmured optimistically, 'and
discover what all this queer business means.'

His prophecy was wrong. The grim and
lonely moor in the region of Crag Fell
was the stage on which Fate had chosen
to play out the end of the drama, the final
scenes of which were at that moment
being set.

13

The raid

In the vault-like chamber beneath the vast warehouse four people were grouped round the bound and helpless forms of two others who lay upon the flagged floor.

'It's useless to continue this obstinacy, Wingate,' said The Gentleman, peering down through the slits m his mask. 'The sooner you realize it the better. I've gone to a considerable amount of trouble and expense and incurred no little risk in order to obtain what I want. And I have no intention of being baulked at the last moment by any feelings of squeamishness. Unless you do as I ask and comply with my demands I shall not hesitate to carry out my threat. My little experiment with your daughter was unfortunately interrupted before, but I assure you that this time there will be no interruption.

This place is ideal for the purpose. The loudest scream could not be heard.'

Deeks who had been listening in silence took a pace forward.

'Can't we cut the cackle and come to the point?' he demanded impatiently. 'Let's get what we want and clear out. I — '

The other swung round on him, his eyes gleaming with cold fury.

'I'm attending to this business!' he snapped. 'When I require your advice I'll ask for it! Now,' he went on, looking down at Wingate, 'for the last time, are you going to tell me what I want to know?'

'No!' replied the convict. 'You can go to hell!'

The Gentleman shrugged his shoulders.

'You're making a fool of yourself,' he said. 'I give you my word that you'll give in, in the end. However, if you prefer to see your daughter suffer rather than speak that's your lookout.'

He took a small case from his pocket and opening it produced the hypodermic syringe. From the same pocket he extracted a bottle filled with colourless fluid.

'I expect you're anxious to see the effects of my experiment,' he went on, setting the bottle on the floor and proceeding to fit the syringe together. 'If that's the case I can assure you they're well worth witnessing. I've only used this method once before and that was only a man. I felt quite sorry for the poor fellow, his screams were appalling.' He screwed the needle into the syringe and uncorking the bottle drew back the plunger. 'Now,' he said when the barrel was full, 'undo Miss Wingate's wrists, Kirk, will you, and bare her arm — right up to the shoulder.'

The red-faced man grinned and carried out the order. Wingate glared, the veins in his temple swelled, but he remained silent. The girl's eyes were dark with fear and her face was chalk-like in its whiteness, but she uttered no word.

'So that you will be able to appreciate what is going to happen,' said The Gentleman, 'you'd better know what this contains.' He held up the syringe and twisted it about in his fingers. 'It contains sulphuric acid, which is commonly called vitriol. When shot into the veins of the patient it produces the most exquisite agony. It's my idea, and I have not, up till now, been able to witness its full effects. The man I tried it on before very inconsiderately went mad after the fourth injection . . . '

'You brute!' burst from Wingate's now bloodless lips. 'You dare to use that infernal stuff!' The words choked in his excess of fury and he strained anxiously at his bonds.

'I not only dare but I shall!' retorted The Gentleman calmly, 'unless you're prepared to do what I ask you.'

The man on the floor remained silent.

'Very well.' The masked man went over to the girl. 'Watch, Wingate,' he said. 'Watch and listen!'

Her eyes dilated with terror as he approached and bent over her, and as he raised her white arm a cry broke from her lips.

'Oh, don't — please don't!' she begged.

The appeal broke down the last

barriers to Wingate's resolve.

'Stop!' he cried harshly. 'You've won, damn you!'

The Gentleman paused with the needle of the syringe touching the soft flesh.

'I thought you'd see reason,' he said. 'Now then, quick, tell me!'

'The Devil's Footprint,' muttered Wingate. 'Give me a piece of paper and I'll show you where.'

'Untie his hands,' ordered The Gentleman, and Kirk obeyed.

'Here's a piece of paper and a pencil,' said Deeks, thrusting his hand in his pocket, and these were given to the helpless man.

He moved his cramped fingers about to restore the circulation, and then placing the sheet of paper on the floor began to draw slowly, pausing every now and then to frown, while Deeks stood above him, watching with glistening, greedy eyes.

'There you are!' he said at last, flinging the pencil away savagely. 'Are you satisfied now?'

'Quite!' said The Gentleman, stepping swiftly forward and picking up the paper.

'Now I suppose you'll release us,' said Wingate.

'Hardly,' said the other as he put the sheet in his pocket. 'That would be a very foolish proceeding. The river flows underneath here and there's a very convenient trap in the other vault. Suitably weighted you and your daughter should lie undisturbed for a considerable time . . . '

'You double-crossing swine!' exclaimed Wingate. 'You promised if I told you what you wanted we should go free!'

'I said nothing of the kind,' The Gentleman reminded him. 'I merely threatened what I would do if you didn't comply with my request. A totally different thing.'

The convict roared and cursed, pleaded and threatened, but without result.

'Bind and gag the pair of them!' snapped The Gentleman. 'Then fetch those weights from the warehouse. Come on, hurry!'

'What are you going to do after?' Deeks inquired.

'I'm going back to Crag Fell,' said the other.

'I don't think you are,' murmured a voice gently. 'You're coming back to Cannon Row with me.'

With a snarl the masked man swung round, and then his jaw dropped. Standing on the threshold was Mr. Budd, his eyes half closed, his lips set, and in his hand the ugly, squat, shape of an automatic.

'Didn't expect to see me, eh?' he remarked smoothly. 'No, don't move, Deeks,' as the ex-valet's hand strayed to his pocket. 'I'm a pretty good shot and I usually shoot through the stomach, it takes a man longer to die that way! Now, put up your hands! You don't stand a chance of gettin' away. The place is surrounded by police.'

Silence greeted his words. The Gentleman slowly raised his hands above his head, glaring concentrated hatred through the slits in his mask.

'Come along in, Mr. Ware, will you?' called the stout Superintendent, 'and give me a hand with this bunch.'

'Coming,' answered Tony, and at that moment The Gentleman made a desperate bid for liberty.

He had been standing less than a foot away from where the dangling light globe hung suspended from its slender wire. Suddenly and without warning of his intention, he sprang forward, clutched the fragile bulb and pulled with all his might.

The flex broke and the light went out, plunging the vault into darkness!

The muzzle of Mr. Budd's automatic spewed jets of flame, the reports were deafening. He had automatically pressed the trigger as the light went out but he realized that the chance of hitting his quarry was microscopic.

Springing forward he called to Tony and the police sergeant who was with him. He heard their answering voices as he cannoned into somebody. It was Deeks' voice that cried out, and clubbing his pistol he struck out blindly. The butt of the weapon thudded on bone and the man fell to the floor.

A beam of light split the blackness as somebody switched on a torch and looking round Mr. Budd saw Tony holding the red-faced man in an unpleasant strangle-hold, and the police sergeant struggling with the liveried chauffeur. The man was fighting like a demon, foaming at the mouth and kicking. The big man came up behind him, gripped him by the collar, almost strangling him, and jerked him backwards. The police officer dragged a pair of handcuffs from his pocket and deftly snapped them on the chauffeur's wrists.

'That's the lot, isn't it?' he panted.

'All except the principal person concerned,' grunted Mr. Budd bitterly. 'He's got away somehow.' He looked quickly round while the other plainclothes man fanned the light of the torch into the corner of the vault.

'There's a door here,' said Mr, Budd, going over to the far corner. 'This is the way he must have gone.'

He thrust against the narrow door.

'Lend a hand here, will you, and we'll see if we can get it open.'

He flung himself against the barrier and felt it give a little. The sergeant joined him and under their combined weight the bolt's socket gave way and the door crashed open.

'There's a passage at the end here,' he said. 'We'll see where it leads.'

They searched the passage and found the exit, a rusty iron ladder that disappeared into the darkness above. It led up to a trap door that opened into a small room inside the warehouse that had obviously been some kind of machine room, probably a lighting power plant or a pumping station. A door at one side stood open leading on to the wharf. Evidently this was the way The Gentleman had escaped.

Mr. Budd came back gloomily to the vault.

'Well, we've got Wingate, anyhow,' he muttered. 'And these other three fellers.' He looked down at the convict sleepily. 'We'll get you and your daughter out of this place, and then I think you and me had better have a chat.'

The man nodded.

'I think so, too,' he said.

14

The Devil's Footprint

The violet haze of evening crept across the melancholy expanse of the moor, lending to the grim heaps of rock and massive crags an illusion of unreality. Over the dark water, which was called the Devil's Footprint a faint white mist hung, looking curiously as though the water was boiling and this was the steam.

In an upstairs window of Crag Fell a single light shone steadily, but otherwise the rambling house was in darkness. The coming night would be moonless. Across the sky low clouds, leaden-hued and threatening, gave promise of rain before morning.

The man who was making his way slowly along the moorland road stared up into the grey vault above him. His mind was too occupied with his own thoughts to concern himself very much about the weather. It had been touch and go in the warehouse, but he had managed to get away, and now, after all his trouble, he was within measurable distance of his reward.

How lucky that fat fool hadn't come a few seconds before — he had been able to extract the information he required from Wingate first. Without it all his plans would have fallen to the ground. Nobody could hope to discover a particular and unknown spot in that vast track of desolate land without knowing exactly where to look.

The Devil's Footprint! So that's where old Ware and Wingate had cached the fortune that they had brought back from abroad. Somewhere hidden in the depths of that two-mile stretch of black and silent water; without definite knowledge it was as secure as a safe deposit.

He increased his pace, and there was greed in his eyes. In his pocket was the rough pencilled sketch Wingate had made showing the exact spot where the chain was anchored; a chain that at the other end held a fortune.

Even had he known that the Devil's

Footprint concealed that of which he was in search it would have been an almost impossible task without that map. Deeks, like the fool he was, had killed old Ware without making sure of his information first. That was what had made him seek out someone to help, for Wingate was the only other person who knew its whereabouts, and it was too big a job for the ex-valet to get him out of prison in order that he could be forced to speak.

The Gentleman had been promised a half share. His lips curled in a smile. That fat detective's intervention in the vault had been profitable after all, for now Deeks and the rest were out of it. He could take the lot for himself!

Not that he had ever intended splitting the stuff with the valet. There would have been a slight accident, a stumble perhaps and an accidental push and Deeks — well —

It was said in the district that the Devil's Footprint was bottomless!

He was nearing his destination now. He left the road and began to cross the rough, uneven surface of the moor towards the vast crags that partly circled his objective.

He stumbled on at an increased pace and presently came to the edge of the still and silent sheet of water. There it lay at his feet, that peculiar-shaped natural lake, without a ripple on its ebon surface.

From his pocket he took the sheet of paper on which Wingate had made his sketch and with the aid of a torch consulted it. There was the mark, a tiny cross at the bend of the heel.

He began to make his way towards the place, skirting the edge of the lake, and presently he came to it. Kneeling he rolled up his right sleeve and plunged his hand and arm into the icy water. Somewhere within a few feet he ought to come upon the staple in the rock to which the chain was attached. He felt about, his hand and fingers growing numb with the cold, and then suddenly he uttered a cry of triumph as they touched something slimy that stretched away into the depths.

His hand closed on it. A chain! He pulled, but it refused to give and he had to use both hands before he could feel any movement. The perspiration was pouring down his face by the time he had pulled into sight a square, black, iron box.

Panting with excitement he dragged it out of the water and laid it on the bank. The thick chain was attached to a ring welded into the metal. Breathing quickly he examined his find and found a narrow keyhole in the broad side. From his inside pocket he produced a short jemmy-like instrument of hardened steel. The end of this he managed, after a little trouble, to insert under the lid. Throwing his whole weight upon it he pressed. With a crack that sounded like the report of a pistol the lock snapped and the lid flew open. Inside was a second receptacle of thin wood covered thickly with paraffin wax. It took him but a few seconds to break this open, and picking up his torch he flashed its light into the interior and gasped at what he saw.

The light was reflected a thousand-fold in rays of green, blood-red and dazzling white. The box was filled almost to the brim with jewels, diamonds, emeralds, rubies that flashed back sparks of fire . . .

He gazed at them spellbound for a second, and then dropping on his knees he ran his fingers through them letting them trickle slowly back into the box. His eyes were glittering and his face was flushed.

'Mine!' he whispered huskily. 'Mine!'

'A nice little collection,' said a slow, ponderous voice. 'Mr. Ware ought to be very grateful to you for findin' 'em for him.'

The Gentleman swung round, his lips curled back from his teeth in an animal like snarl.

'You!' he grated huskily. 'You!'

'Me!' announced Mr. Budd pleasantly. 'Also Leek, and a few other policemen. I don't think you're going to get away this time.'

The Gentleman glanced quickly about him and saw the shadowy shapes that appeared from behind the rocks.

'You win!' he said thickly. 'I knew you'd get here but I never thought it would be so soon. I thought I just had time.'

'I've been waitin' for you since this afternoon,' said Mr. Budd, and raising his voice: 'Come and take this feller, Leek.'

The long, thin form of the melancholy sergeant advanced and he was within two feet of the cornered man when he turned suddenly, and before they could prevent him had plunged into the water of the lake.

He sank like a stone, and the ripples circled sluggishly over the black surface. One of the plainclothes men flung off his coat and dived in after him, but he never found him, neither was he ever seen again. Whether the icy waters of the Devil's Footprint were bottomless or not somewhere in the depths the body of The Gentleman remained forever.

For although when the daylight came the lake was dragged nothing was brought to the surface.

* * *

'Now, let's hear all about it, Budd,' said Tony, stretching out his feet to the roaring fire in the dining room at Crag Fell. 'What was at the bottom of all this business? Those jewels?'

275

Mr. Budd finished carefully lighting a cigar and nodded.

'Yes,' he answered. 'Accordin' to Wingate he and your uncle were on an explorin' expedition when they came across a clue relatin' to a hoard of treasure buried by the Incas. The place was somewhere on the Rollito River, and they decided to see if there was anythin' in it. They seemed to have had some pretty interestin' adventures before they finally located the treasure, but that's nothin' to do with this business. They did find it and returned with it to Brazil. If they'd let it become known that in their baggage was somethin' like half a million pounds worth of jewels their lives wouldn't have been worth anythin'. So they said nothin' to nobody. Their servant who was in their confidence and who had been with them on the expedition was taken ill and died in Brazil, and your uncle took on in his place a starvin' Englishman named Deeks, who had asked for help.

'Wingate, Ware and this feller returned to England with the jewels. Your uncle suggested that until they found suitable buyers, these stones were too big to sell in the ordinary market, the jewels should be hidden in a box and sunk in the Devil's Footprint. Bein' a traveller he didn't know much about banks and safe-deposits and rather distrusted them, bein' more used to looking after himself. Deeks came to hear about the jewels, and learned, probably by listenin' at keyholes, that they were hidden somewhere on the Moor, and he thought they'd make a very nice present for himself if he could get hold of 'em.

'He was under the impression that some sort of map or chart was in existence showin' where they was hidden, and he probably got this in his head from hearin' your uncle and Wingate discussin' the map which had originally led them to the treasure.

'He was caught by your uncle one day searchin' his desk and an argument ensued. He followed your uncle on to the moor, high words led to blows and your uncle fell backwards over the quarry and broke his neck — at least that's Deek's version. Whether he was deliberately murdered I don't know, but I'm inclined to think he was.

'Deeks searched the body, and was dismayed to find that there was nothing showing the whereabouts of the treasure, but he wasn't going to give up a fortune without a struggle.

'Unfortunately Wingate by this time was in prison, and he was the only feller besides your uncle who knew where the jewels was. Deeks, who was a pretty bad hat, knew most of the undesirables and enlisted, through Kirk, the help of The Gentleman, with what result you know.'

'It seems pretty clear,' remarked Tony as the other paused. 'How did they get hold of the girl?'

'Found she was livin' in Kensington with an aunt, and pitched a yarn about bein' friends of her father's and havin' a scheme to help him escape,' replied Mr. Budd with a prodigious yawn. 'Of course, she jumped at the idea. They told her some story about Wingate bein' able to establish his innocence if he could get free for a few days. It was The

Gentleman's plan that they should have her at hand in case Wingate should prove difficult.'

Tony frowned.

'What about the man he shot?' he inquired. 'What was his name — Spaken. How does he come into it?'

'He doesn't!' replied the fat detective. 'He knew somethin' about Wingate's wife before he married her and threatened to make it public unless Wingate paid him to keep silent. He was just a blackmailer, that's all. Wingate lost his temper, he had already paid the best part of three thousand pounds, and refused to hand over any more money. Spakin, in a rage, sprang at him in the drive of his house in Sussex. Wingate shot him in self-defence with the gun he succeeded in wrenching from Spaken. That's his own story and I believe him. He couldn't divulge the reason before because it would have affected his wife's reputation, so he kept silent at his trial. She's dead now though, and when the true facts are placed before the Home Secretary I don't suppose there'll be much doubt about him getting an early pardon.'

'Well, that's good news, anyway,' said Tony and then his face clouded. 'Poor Old Kessick,' he said. 'I wonder what happened to him?'

'I've got an idea that his body is somewhere in the Devil's Footprint,' said Mr. Budd, 'along with the man who took his place. It was a clever bit of work on The Gentleman's part that, impersonatin' the old man, and not difficult seein' as how you hadn't seen him for twelve years.'

'I can't understand,' said Tony, 'how his own son could have lent himself to the murder of his father, if that's what happened.'

'I expect,' said the Superintendent, 'he was told that it was an accident. He may have suspected it wasn't, but was too frightened to do much. They 'ad some sort of a hold on him, and probably promised him a good share of the treasure when it was found.'

He yawned again.

'Of course, it was Deeks who played ghosts on you. He knew about the hidden room, and The Gentleman decided that it would be a good place to bring Wingate when they got him out of prison. It's only a theory of mine, but I believe he had at the back of his mind that this house, bein' lonely and solitary-like, would make a good headquarters, after they'd got you out of the way.'

He took a long pull at his cigar and blew a cloud of smoke towards the ceiling.

'Well, it's all over now,' he said. 'It's been a pretty wearin' time. I don't think Leek's put in so much real work for years.'

The lugubrious sergeant raised his eyes mournfully

'I ought to be pensioned off,' he said. 'I've had a severe shock to my system and it'll take me a long time to recover.'

'You've been as good as pensioned off ever since you joined the force!' grunted Mr. Budd, and then going off at a tangent: 'That's a nice girl, Mr. Ware. It's a long time since I've seen a prettier.'

Tony reddened.

'What made you say that?' he demanded.

'I dunno,' murmured Mr. Budd. 'I was just thinkin'. I'm naturally romantic!'

THE END

We do hope that you have enjoyed reading this large print book.

Did you know that all of our titles are available for purchase?

We publish a wide range of high quality large print books including:

Romances, Mysteries, Classics
General Fiction
Non Fiction and Westerns

Special interest titles available in large print are:

The Little Oxford Dictionary
Music Book, Song Book
Hymn Book, Service Book

Also available from us courtesy of Oxford University Press:

Young Readers' Dictionary
(large print edition)
Young Readers' Thesaurus
(large print edition)

For further information or a free brochure, please contact us at:
Ulverscroft Large Print Books Ltd.,
The Green, Bradgate Road, Anstey,
Leicester, LE7 7FU, England.
Tel: (00 44) **0116 236 4325**
Fax: (00 44) **0116 234 0205**

Other titles in the
Linford Mystery Library:

MARKED FOR MURDER

Norman Lazenby

'Leave this affair alone, Martinson — Jean Hallison is dead . . . ' The caller had rung off, leaving Inspector Jim Martinson wondering if this was a bluff. Had Jean been murdered? And where did the suave, grinning Montoni fit in? He was accused of assaulting two women — but at the same time Jim himself had been watching him elsewhere. Now, however, Jim links the chain of evidence — slowly tightening the rope that will bring in the sinister gang that is terrorising Framcastle.

BURY THE HATCHET

John Russell Fearn

George Carter and his family lived peacefully in the small town of Uphill. But one fateful weekend something caused them to experience real fear and act completely out of character. The first trigger was when they learned that a homicidal maniac was at large in Uphill, carrying a damaged suitcase containing his victim's body parts. The second trigger was on finding that their new lodger's suitcase was also damaged — and the grisly truth of what was inside . . .

EXPERIMENT IN MURDER

John Russell Fearn

Moore dreams he's in the Lake District, climbing a mountain — carrying a woman's body — the woman he attacked as she slept in their hotel. He throws her body into the chasm at the summit and returns to the hotel. He wakes up. He examines his shoes: just as he left them before retiring, no trace of mud from the hillside . . . then it HAS all been a dream! But Moore, victim of an experiment in murder, finds his dream is real!

KILLER SMILE

Steve Hayes & David Whitehead

Jack Monroe's dream was to start a foundation that would encourage architects from poorer families. But to achieve this dream he would need fifty million dollars. So he hooked up with the wealthy Thornhill family. But the Thornhills had more than their share of dirty secrets, and Jack found himself a pawn in a deadly game of murder and deceit. Now, he would need to take the utmost care not to become the architect of his own downfall.

MR. BUDD STEPS IN

Gerald Verner

Somewhere in England is a steel box — its contents more valuable than diamonds — that Superintendent Robert Budd must find. Budd's investigation takes him to Higher Wicklow, where a tramp had sheltered in its reputedly haunted mill. Some days later, his body was discovered, his throat cut. Although the coroner's verdict was suicide, the villagers believe there's a more sinister explanation. Can the Superintendent discover the truth? Budd's heavy caseload also includes murder, ghostly goings on, a vanishing and blackmail.

THE DARK GATEWAY

John Burke

In a lonely corner of Wales, an ancient castle quivers with evil as menacing powers return from beyond . . . The family living on the hillside farm with their daughter, Nora, has a stranger coming to live with them. But he's not what he seems — he will not fulfil Nora's hopes of romance . . . As the powers of darkness approach, the human race is in danger and the earth itself is at stake. In this frightened community, who will oppose the invaders?